THE
MAIDENSTONE

A MURDER MYSTERY

Anne Gumley

Order this book online at www.trafford.com
or email orders@trafford.com

Most Trafford titles are also available at major online book retailers.

Printed in the United States of America.

ISBN: 978-1-4669-7775-4 (sc)
ISBN: 978-1-4669-7776-1 (hc)
ISBN: 978-1-4669-7777-8 (e)

Library of Congress Control Number: 2013901167

Trafford rev. 03/22/2013

 www.trafford.com

North America & international
toll-free: 1 888 232 4444 (USA & Canada)
phone: 250 383 6864 ♦ fax: 812 355 4082

To Don.
For keeping me in touch with my roots

Prologue—2500 B.C.

The land that rose gently to the Eastern side of the Pennine Chain had changed gradually over the last decade. Warmer than normal breezes blew over the soft sand deposits of what was once a salt sea, that had over time changed into small lakes and eventually became peat bogs. The once green grass and reeds that had sprung up around them now struggled to exist. Climate change had left its mark, and the inhabitants that had long ago settled there were feeling its effects.

A small party of Neolithic people trod a well worn path along the edge of the Pennines. Their clothes were simple, mostly skins and rough woven cloth. The group added up to no more than a dozen, as they panted for breath; the sun giving little relief as it hung overhead in a cloudless sky. Their route took them away from the small settlement of rectangular log houses in the valley below where the land had been painfully cleared for crops of oats and wheat. Now however it only supported their exhausted cattle and pigs. Here and there a murder of crows covered a carcass like a black cloak. The dry earth waited for the rain that had once been the source of their existence. The God of the Clouds had once looked after them well, but after a number of seasons of his unwillingness to help, something needed to be done, and the only way to appease the God was through sacrifice.

The young girl that was being dragged along by the group was no more than eight summers. The rope that had been placed around her neck was made of horse hair, and each time her step faltered along the stony ridge, it was pulled; making her stumble again.

Fortunately she didn't feel pain; there was only a deep relaxation in her body and an empty space in her head, as though she was watching herself from a distance.

The man who led the group breathed heavily, the animal skin around his shoulders rubbed his damp skin and the amber stones and animal bones of his headdress picked at his skin. But like the girl; he too was oblivious to pain after drinking from the polished skull.

He climbed steadily, an excitement growing with each step. Spittle dribbled from one corner of his mouth. He sucked it in eagerly to moisten his dry throat. Nearly there, his steps quickened as the grey standing stone came into view. The pile of earth dug out in front made him shiver with anticipation.

Suddenly a small cry from behind him was heard, and a faint intake of breath came from one of the group. His excitement grew; the drug was wearing off as it should, for the exact amount was crucial, and he was well aware of its potency.

The God of the Clouds would reward him well.

All at once the girl began to experience a slight tingling through her frame; her mouth was too dry to swallow. She felt the stinging of her flesh as the rope bit in. Panic surged up as her mind cleared, she opened her mouth to cry out but nothing came; just a choking sound.

Someone behind her gave a little sob of distress, then rough hands pushed her forward up the last incline and she was standing in front of a huge grey stone, her heels tipping slightly to the edge of a dark hole in front of it.

She looked up; the skies had darkened as clouds rolled in, a large black raven circled above. Then she was looking into the frenzied eyes of the priest, his face distorted in a manic ecstasy of pure pleasure. She saw the swift motion of an arm raised, and then total oblivion, as her small tender body shuddered with the rock's impact against her head.

Her body fell. She slid to the ground, blood washing her limbs as the head split open. The priest stood totally still; his body still feeling the ecstasy that cruised through his body as the stone hit the victim. The girl was laid on her side, a jar of food placed by her body. Willing hands covered her with soil.

As the chanting began, the priest raised his head and hands to the sky and the gods that lived there. Suddenly there was a flash of lightening and a crash of thunder. The clouds burst open and the rains fell. The sacrifice was offered and the God of the Clouds was pleased.

Now the settlement could survive; and they would live to cultivate the land.

Chapter 1

The Edge 1996

He firmly believed in fate. You couldn't control it or plan for it. It just happened.

One moment life was hum-drum and uneventful; then changed in the twinkling of an eye.

It had been like this all his life. Just one boring day after another, then out of the blue, something presented itself that pushed his hormones to the point of ecstasy.

He'd wondered sometimes whether he had some Divine spark in him. He couldn't share his experiences with anyone; he knew that they wouldn't understand. How could they, for to truly understand one had to have direct experience, and the experience could get them into a lot of trouble.

He was different and gifted, probably again by Divine intervention. Chosen? He'd sometimes contemplated on the fact but then thought it too self-righteous. Humble was better. Being humble and waiting for that special moment was the right way to go. He had patience; lots of it in fact. It was a source of pride.

However five years of patience awaiting fate was a long time to wait, and at times he felt some of it running out. As he watched the slim figure striding out ahead of him, he felt almost guilty of not disciplining his gift more; coupled with the fact his body was on the verge of exploding with joy.

Over the years he'd had an occasional joint, popped a pill or two: never purchased mind, always given freely at some party or other. However always disappointed; none of the artificial stuff gave him the high which fate brought him.

It was as if an inner flame had been lit as he watched the slim figure walking ahead of him. How could he have known what the day awaited as he showered and shaved that morning? Coffee and toast and his morning stroll up the lane. He always stopped at the cross-roads turned back and came home.

This morning was different, having reached the cross-roads he didn't turn around, but for some unknown reason he would later call fate; he kept on walking.

He walked along the narrow lane that turned off to the right, climbed over the style and continued. It was as if his feet had a mind of their own. He thought he felt something stir within his chest, a quickening of his heartbeat perhaps. His memory pushed to be released; too long held under control. He didn't know whether the first encounter with that powerful surge of excitement he at once felt could be controlled. Everything around him reminded him of it.

Even the brooding skies and morning shadows claimed the shapes of long ago. The Cheshire plains spread out before him at the end of the Pennines, known as the backbone of England.

The ground beneath his feet had also been trampled on by Neolithic and Bronze Age people alike; though then peat bogs and later marsh lands, before the oaks, ash and birch trees took root and the woodland gave shelter to wild animals. Most likely the land would have been cleared and crops of oats and wheat would have swayed in the breeze.

Now the land was left to its own devices and the gentler of the animal species and birds flourished. No one hunted there, although rabbits were a common sight as were pheasants and partridge.

An occasional fox or badger was sighted but overall the land took on the appearance of the moorland of the nearby Buxton area. Not so windswept or isolated for if one looked south the tops of buildings and the occasional string electrical pylons could be seen.

The Edge, as it was known by, had its own artefacts and history that brought forth archaeologists to the area from time to time. A Neolithic tomb had been found, its giant slabs of stone protecting the dead, had been hewn from the nearby rock face. A huge nearby burial mound had produced burnt human bones and charcoal remains indicating that people had been cremated.

Spearheads and axes plus Roman coins found their way into the local museum and most likely many more were hidden at the back of drawers in the homes of local people.

For the students of archaeology and like minded people these all held interest and from time to time groups could be seen with note books and cameras.

Yet the site that held the most interest was a solitary burial site known locally as the Maidenstone.

It consisted of a tall stone leaning awkwardly to the right, bearing strange symbols not yet interpreted and thought by the powers that be; to be pagan ritual signs. In the late eighteen hundreds, the site had been excavated under the stone and the remains of a young girl found together with an earthenware jar, holding three strangely carved figures. Such a find that had brought about a great deal of excitement, together with a well-preserved lock of auburn hair and a skull that had been badly damaged on one side. With a later investigation after the Second World War, it had been decided that the person was about eight years old and had been killed by a blow to the side of the head.

Whether it was intentional or accidental couldn't be truly established, but owing to the manner of the burial and the objects around her, it was unanimously voted as a ritual death. This was all very interesting and promoted an occasional cult gathering on the eve of a full moon or some other special cult ceremony.

However the most talked about event regarding the Maidenstone, was a more recent death. Recent in terms of the twentieth century, although in truth the murder had happened some thirty years ago.

It was the discovery of a ten year old girl whose skull had been fractured causing death.

The murderer was never found and the mystery remained leading to the myth of a sacrificial death. Occasionally a few flowers, picked from nearby, would be found placed at the foot of the stone, as if someone felt the souls of the two girls centuries apart were crying out, or maybe it was just a nice thing to do. Today a few dried petals of daisies lay scattered under the stone's shadow.

The man whose feet were taking him in the direction of the Maidenstone was too far away to see it, although has gaze was concentrated in its direction. He'd just climbed the rise in the land before getting its panoramic view. He stopped momentarily as did his breath. An overwhelming cry of joy stopped short of being released but he felt its tingling and buzzing in his ears. Ahead of him, walking at a slow but purposeful pace was a figure. For a second he couldn't move; like the time he'd taken pot, and his body seemed separated from his mind.

The figure ahead was a female, the walk was full of energy and purpose, her hair lifted by the breeze seemed to dance. A bag with a long strap bounced against her leg as it was carried in one hand and swayed with her rhythm.

It was like going back in time. He quickened his step, careful to avoid anything that might disturb the silence.

Running was out of the question much as the pressure inside him wanted him to do.

Silently calculating the make up of the distance between them, and instinctively knowing where she was heading he lengthened his strides.

Energy flowed through his body; every nerve was awakened and ready for action. The surging up of incredible excitement ran though his veins, making him almost dizzy. Occasionally he'd experience the release of his sexual hormones, but although it was satisfactory, nothing could hold a candle to what was building up inside him.

Suddenly his breath seemed to be released with one long out-breath; then normalized. The Maidenstone had come into view, its lob-sided form looking at odds with its surroundings.

The figure in front of him turned. She'd seen him and looked apprehensive. He gave a short salute and shaded his eyes, as if scanning the land around for birds. She relaxed and slowed down, maybe she knew him, or had a common interest in the area. Taking out a note book and a chewed pencil from her anorak, she started the steady climb up to the Maidenstone.

By the time he'd caught up with her she was half kneeling, holding a magnifying glass against the stone pillar, in an attempt to see the symbols more clearly. There was no way she could interpret the markings, even the best archaeologist had failed to do that, but it was a good subject for her exams; the powers that be had said use your imagination, and yes this was the perfect place to compose an essay on rituals.

She looked sideways at the figure of a man coming towards her. Maybe he was familiar with the Maidenstone and could give her some tips. He looked local and obviously knew the land around.

She saw him bend down and pick something up and wondered if he'd found something of interest. Two minutes later she felt his presence behind her and turned.

His face was lit up, his whole countenance radiating excitement. His body was trembling. He's found something, was her first and last thought as he raised his hand as if to show her. Her eyes followed puzzled, his arm too high and his hand holding a rock of some sort.

She didn't have time to question. The sudden explosion caused extreme pain . . . . , then nothing.

Chapter 2

Police Sergeant Jack Buzzard shifted his position on the hard steel-backed chair. Immediately he felt the warm flow of blood as he straightened his legs and crossed his ankles. A forward slip of his body promoted a lifting of arms and hands to fold behind his head. In a position of ease, he surveyed the square box before him. The dark computer screen in front of it reflected his image, and he turned slightly to evaluate his balding patch.

'Never too late,' his friend had encouraged recently as they sat side by side on the settee reading an advertisement for hair pieces. Naturally they had both laughed; vanity wasn't for the nearly sixty plus in age. Yet Jack felt drawn to the idea of starting his coming retirement with a positive attitude. One never knew who one would meet, although he had little interest in the female species.

He leaned forward, picked up a pen and twirled it between his fingers, an old habit he'd perfected as a child. His mind skipping often into the past to a time before the advent of computers: A time when the stress of work didn't happen so frequently. Now re-learning seemed to occupy most of his day as he wrestled with the new technology.

He sniffed loudly, a habit of a lifetime when coming to terms with his own abilities. Retirement would come as a blessing; convinced he'd never get the hang of the computer. The pencil fell from his fingers onto the floor and rolled under the chair. Picking it up and regaining his position, his mind leapt to the next coming months and wondered if any plans for his retirement were underway.

The ending of his career had come slowly and quietly like a thief in the night. In less than six months his working life would end.

His hand went to his mouth, his thumb nail clicking against his teeth. No doubt at all a retirement get together would be in the offing, plenty of sandwiches, probably salmon and cucumber as always, a cake of course, baked at the local supermarket with his name iced on it at the last moment. Then there was the presentation to follow; keeping in mind the retiree's hobbies.

Jack paused . . . . He didn't have any hobbies as such. TV was the only thing he placed of importance in his single life and he'd already got one.

His muscles around his mouth pulled it into a long line that was neither a smile nor a scorn; just indifference to any thoughts that popped up. Only thing for sure, the speech on his career wouldn't last long; that ladder had only two steps as far as he was concerned, but they had been good enough for his father and grandfather before him.

Maybe someone would mention he had actually been in the Investigation Division, and was a detective constable for a time. Heath would have certainly remembered, and for a brief second his spirits lightened only to be replaced by a sigh as he remembered Ernest Heath, a retired detective inspector, would probably not be there.

His mind dipped into another past pathway of memories. Ernest Heath and he had joined the force at the same time. Heath; the name slipped silently off Jack's tongue. There was a person who knew where he was going, with his brooding eyes and handsome face. Sergeant Buzzard half closed his eyes and brought up a face that still stirred an emotion in him which he'd learned to repress over the years.

Then his whole body relaxed and he almost drifted off into a catnap. However he was rudely awakened by the phone ringing on the front desk. He leapt up, nearly falling over his chair in his effort to reach it.

'Danesbury Police Headquarters,' his voice became automatic and professional. There was a rush of breath being exhaled, followed by the hiss of an in-breath. The words came out quickly with a hint of hysteria.

'There's a young girl . . . . , dead. Oh it's awful.' The voice trailed off suddenly with what sounded like a choke. The full force of the sergeant's experience came to bear; his voice controlled and purposeful.

'Take your time sir; I'm listening.'

The calm voice seemed to give the caller some assurance and he could be heard taking a deep breath.

'I've just found a young girl with her head bashed in; lying by the Maidenstone on the Edge.' A choke again . . . , then; 'God, it is awful.'

Sergeant Buzzard slid a pad and pencil towards him and pressed record on the phone; training had taught him to be detached and get details.

'Where are you phoning from sir, and what is your name and address?'

There was a moment of silence, but when the answer came back it was less hysterical.

'I'm phoning from the phone box at the bottom of Stags Lane. I went bird watching on the Edge and found,' the voice quivered a little with the recall. 'She looked so young; what was left of her face. God it was horrible . . . . My name is Ivan Banes.'

Sergeant Buzzard's writing flew over the page, before telling the caller not to move and someone would pick him up shortly. The response was again another choking sound as the phone was replaced.

Police vehicles raced through the heart of the town with sirens blowing; followed by an ambulance. Pedestrians stood transfixed watching the convoy, or if jay-walking, leaping quickly onto the safety of the pavements; their minds all contemplating the worst of scenarios.

It took very little time to reach the phone booth, and without ceremony, the young man, standing white-faced outside the booth, was bundled into the leading car.

Having decided that the informant knew the Edge well and could cut down the time needed to reach the scene of the crime, he found himself having once again to face his worst nightmare.

However, now confronted by the presence of the men in uniform around, his confidence began to return with a certain sense of excitement building within. He glanced at the photographer giving a slight smile, indicating he didn't mind having his photo taken. He even began to contemplate the amount the papers paid for information like this.

Puffed a little by his growing importance, he strode out along the route he'd taken earlier. His legs were well accustomed to the terrain of rocks and crevices, and he secretly enjoyed the stumbles and heavy breathing of his police companions following closely behind.

The only time his nerve nearly failed was as they came in sight of the old Bronze Age stone, and what looked like a bundle of rags beneath it.

He pointed to the stone known as the Maidenstone, feeling an acid reflux beginning to rise from his stomach, and was thankful a strong arm stopped him from going any further.

'Alright son?' Detective Chief Inspector Granger placed has steady hand under his elbow. 'Is this how you found her?'

The question seemed silly at first, until the chief went on to ask; 'nothing changed?'

Ivan shook his head; he would remember every detail for the rest of his life.

Detective Chief Inspector Granger turned and nodded to the police surgeon who knelt down by the victim to quickly establish the time of death. Finger prints were taken, everything bagged by the Crime Scene Officers and the body carefully lifted and zipped into a green plastic bag, after the photographer had taken photos from every angle.

Detective Chief Inspector Granger stepped back and awaited the doctor to join him. The round bald head of Dr. Grimshaw shook.

'Not more than age ten I'd say, killed by a blow to the head.' He sighed and looked over to the SOCO officers. 'We have the murder weapon. She was hit by a rock.'

'So probably an unplanned killing,' mused Granger.

He then looked up. 'Any sexual interference?'

The doctor glanced up at the taller man. 'Can't detect any signs.' He stopped and looked over at the body being lifted onto the stretcher, 'but better to make that final assumption after the examination back at the morgue.'

D.C.I Granger nodded, his mouth felt dry and the coffee he'd left behind flicked through his mind. He gave the doctor a pat on the back before turning.

'I'm off then; reckon I'll not get much sleep for a while yet.'

The walk back seemed longer, the adrenaline playing itself out. He followed the group of men, leaving a stoned-faced constable by the scene of the crime looking slightly dismayed at the scenery and isolation around him.

A sudden flash of compassion made him call to one of the other constables and indicated he too should stay there; the act endearing him to one, but not the other.

Back at the headquarters, Sergeant Buzzard was ready to greet the incoming activity after a surprising burst of energy. The CID room had been set up with all the necessary equipment for various departments to come together.

The sergeant leaned over the long counter awaiting the homicide teams to enter, trying to recall the details of a much earlier but identical homicide, some thirty years earlier. At that time Ernest Heath was a detective sergeant with a positive future in front of him, and he himself; a detective constable, looking ahead to a career in investigations.

Then it all fell apart. He couldn't quite remember the details but the case was never resolved. Something had happened higher up in the police chain-of-command. One thing he was certain of however; the murderer had never been caught.

Chapter 3

A few miles away in the quiet village of Gelsby, an elderly couple were contemplating the ritual of worship from a different angle.

One look at Rita's face was enough to send a slight flush over her husband's cheeks as he put down the small book he was holding, and slipped a well chewed pencil into his jacket pocket.

She shook her head in mock despair, although as she turned away a slight smile formed. He'd never change, nor did she ever want him to, although in truth there had been many times she'd have willingly thrown his puzzles and crosswords on the fire.

Rita glanced at her watch. She never noticed that the glass was scratched and the leather strap cracked. It had served her well though her nursing career and she didn't need to change it.

A frown formed on her forehead. It was quarter to the hour and she didn't fancy disturbing the morning service by being late. Perhaps it wasn't such a good idea of hers after all, persuading Lisa that her mother would be pleased. After all Lisa's mother was very much dead. Rita sighed, and heard Ernest cough. The sound produced when one is unsure of what's expected and a little tired of just hanging around.

She turned a little, half taking in her husband's solid figure, and as always, felt an immediate and overwhelming wonderment of them being together.

A continent away and half a life time had separated them. Then out of the blue, which Ernest called fate; they had met again. What they had felt for each other in their early years had left a flame that had never been put out.

Ernest Heath, her childhood sweetheart was now her husband and each morning their hands would find the other's in bed and grasped each other to make sure it wasn't all a dream.

A moment of regret at her insistence on accompanying Lisa to church overwhelmed Rita for she was well aware of Ernest's view on religion from his earlier life at the church school they both had attended.

Rita felt hot around her neck and pulled at the silk paisley scarf. She was as much a hypocrite herself, for having delivered hundreds of babies; couldn't accept the Immaculate Conception and had always thought it a myth of past generations who didn't understand about eggs and sperm. As for the raising of the dead; a recovery from a cataleptic state could well be the reason for a return to life, but anything else belied her intelligence.

However having reaffirmed the practical reasoning she had from the direct experience of her calling, and knowing that the emotional side of any person is usually the thrust that drives the machine; she was and always had been very sympathetic to this.

Direct experience of life was far above only hearing or reading about it, and Rita had faced her own trials many times. Now Lisa needed her help and if it entailed playing on her vulnerability was the only way, then so be it. However as the seconds passed, Rita was having second thoughts

'Should I go around and fetch her . . . .' Ernest's concerned voice broke Rita's thoughts and for a moment she hesitated;

but remained looking at Ernest with the same steadfastness he'd come to appreciate and expect of her.

'No love.' Rita sat down by the kitchen table. 'Best let her make that decision herself.'

Ernest nodded and glanced at the somewhat used puzzle book. 'Maybe you went a little too far by telling her that her dead mother would be happy to see her in church on her birthday.' Ernest spoke the words with hesitation, knowing full well it would never have worked for him.

Rita rolled her neck and half smiled. 'Ernest, if it takes lies to get Lisa out of the house to stop her brooding, I'll do it.'

Ernest nodded again as he recalled the tragic period when Detective Sergeant Lisa Pharies was suspended, following her failure to call for back-up when needed. It had resulted in her own injuries: which thankfully had now mended with time. Ernest, a retired detective inspector himself and both her confidant and neighbour, had felt almost guilty at not being more aware of where Lisa's investigations were heading with that particular case.

The relationship between Lisa and Ernest was much more than just neighbourly, for Detective Sergeant Pharies had previously worked for Ernest when he was a detective inspector and the respect for each other had been long ago cemented. When Ernest retired, Lisa had encouraged him to buy a vacant cottage in Gelsby, two doors away from the one where she had then lived with her infirmed mother.

The village of Gelsby was situated a few miles outside the town of Danesbury where they had both worked, and the rows of old cottages flanked the village green. It was a picturesque village that attracted many sight-seers; especially during the May-time festivities that drew crowds to witness the annual maypole dancing.

The one and only public house in the village was called the Horseshoe. It was built on the side of an old smithy, and catered to wedding parties and the many sight-seers. It was also the local watering hole for the regulars that met there for companionship and gossip.

Overseeing it all was the ancient church of St. Anne's, built originally in the Saxon period and surviving the Reformation with little damage; changing from Roman Catholic to Protestant.

The grand gated entrance and the solid stately tower; the grotesque gargoyles, the guardians that kept away evil spirits, and the sounds of the full-peal of the church bells; calling the faithful to church, and giving the village that ever-presence of being English.

Ernest's retirement was complete when he again found his one and only love Rita, and together they subconsciously adopted Lisa as the child they never had or could have. Ernest had everything he desired; his wife Rita, the sharing of many on-going investigations through Lisa, and his crosswords and puzzles that kept his mind active and alert. Today however his world was tipping a little to unravelling and he felt out of control.

The bell on the front door clanged and broke the silence. They both looked at each other . . . . hopefully. If it was Lisa, it would mean she had at least left the confines of her two bed roomed cottage and stepped outside. Hope raised their spirits and Rita indicated she should be the one to open the door.

To her great relief Lisa stood awkwardly on the doorstep, one hand still hovering near the bell push. She looked somewhat frail, her hair limper than usual, lacking body, and her features pale. Rita noticed she wasn't using her walking stick, which immediately suggested the gun-shot wound in her leg had healed well and left no permanent damage. Lisa half smiled, even if noticeably forced.

'Come on you two, the bells will be deafening us in a few minutes.' The effort at a joke seemed to take the edge off all the concern and Rita bent forward to kiss the cool forehead before her, before shouting to Ernest to hurry up. It was a sobering sight for the parishioners seeing the three climb the steps to the ancient gates, and walk in closed contact along the flagged path to the great west doors.

There were few in the village that didn't feel sympathy for Lisa Pharies. It seemed bad luck was never very far away when it came to her relationships; she'd had two chances at romance. The first had turned out to be her cousin; not to mention his chosen calling to the priesthood. The second was much worse though, as he turned out to be a murderer and was the one that had shot her in the leg.

All this to be followed by her mother's death; and left with no near kin. The villagers shook their heads in a mixture of gossip and sympathy, the latter mostly winning as Lisa Pharies was one of their own, as her ancestors had been, and houses in Gelsby hardly ever came up for sale. Even the council would step away from proposing any new buildings; their term of office usually short and final if they persisted.

It wasn't of course really up to the local council as the church owned most of the land which over the centuries had been rented out to small farm holdings. The name for the church lands were known as glebe lands, so it wasn't surprising that there were farms, houses and roads that had also adopted the glebe name. There was an old rumour that even the Horseshoe Inn had once applied for the name of "Glebe Rest" but it went the way of many other discarded rumours.

So there was a rise and fall of murmuring among the parishioners when Ernest escorted the two women down the side-aisle, allowing them to enter the pew first so that he sat at the end.

Unless it was some big occasion that the grandeur of the building enhanced, the regular morning service saw many empty pews. He'd often contemplated on the fact that no matter how large a space there was, there was always a comfort zone that got filled first. Not that there was much comfort in trying to hear the rector's quiet voice wherever one sat.

Forever analysing, Ernest looked at his own motive that had driven him to find a seat at the end of a pew and behind a large stone pillar that supported the roof that would give him privacy. He patted his pocket to reassure himself and felt the slight crackle of paper and the round hard stub of a pencil.

Ernest knelt, he knew the routine by rote, having been brought up through the Church of England school, not that there had been any choice, apart from becoming a Roman Catholic; these being the only two schools in the town.

His knees cracked as he kneeled, his large hands supporting his head. No one would have guessed that if he prayed for some help it would be to give his grey brain cells a push into enlightenment, not of the spiritual sort but some defining arrangement of figures. He turned slightly and saw Rita take Lisa's hand and give it a squeeze. He felt blessed whatever the reason.

During the service Ernest with long learnt skill had managed to reach into his pocket and place the piece of paper between the pages of the prayer book. However the placing of the pencil in his hand took real skill, but he laid it carefully by his side and as the clues to the page torn from his extra hard Sudoku puzzle book began to be figured out, he managed somehow to write it in. Unfortunately when they stood to sing the pencil rolled and dropped on the stone floor with a slight but unusual noise. Rita heard it, glanced down and saw the pencil and the prayer book's extra page and frowned.

A slight tut escaped her lips, followed by a disappointed shake of her head. Ernest blushed but on kneeling again managed to retrieve the objects and pushed them firmly back into his pocket. Only two hymns to go; and Rita had been singing with gusto.

The sun had come out a little when they left the church, although the air was still quite chilly. Frank Butterworth with his ramrod straight back and arms swinging in a military fashion, was edging his way towards them. Rita saw him first and manoeuvred Lisa away, leaving Ernest to take on the village know-it-all.

'Inspector.' Frank tipped his hand to his forehead.

'Retired.' Ernest reminded him as he always did.

'Quite,' came back the high authoritarian voice, cultured with old-school-boy overtones. 'But once in command; it never leaves one you know.'

Ernest had no reason to take it as a complement, as the retired Major Butterworth was obviously talking about himself. Ahead Lisa and Rita had reached the massive stone archway and were half way down the flagged steps where they had a total view of the triangular village green and the cottages flanking it with their small gardens and rear access road, to and from the road around the church.

About to drop her foot on the third of the six steps, Lisa pulled at Rita's sleeve. They stopped and watched a large black shiny car pull up outside number eleven. A man got out and looked at the house.

'You've got a visitor Rita.' There was a slight regret as if it meant the tea and biscuits might get cancelled and at this point she didn't want to go back to an empty house.

'Do you know him?' Lisa enquired, with a slight frown forming around her eyes. 'He looks familiar.'

'No.' Rita affirmed with conviction, but found herself searching her memory. He did indeed remind her of someone.

Skipping down the remaining steps they hurried forward, but before she could shout, the man had turned as if having second thoughts; got into his car and drove off.

The two women stopped, a little baffled.

'Maybe he'd got the wrong address,' offered Lisa.

'Maybe,' came back the answer. Yet she couldn't get rid of the feeling she knew him. There was something else that reminded her of someone she knew.

Chapter 4

'Maybe he had the wrong address,' offered Lisa shrugging her shoulders as if it was an everyday occurrence.

'Hmm.' Ernest mumbled, catching up with them and hearing about the visitor.

'Thanks for the input,' said Rita a trifle sarcastically.

'Was he the only person in the car?' asked Ernest, with a slight scowl of impatience; as if he couldn't quite understand why they hadn't used their observational skills.

Lisa sighed, while Rita frowned. It was these small things that always made Lisa feel she would never make the grade in her chosen profession. She sighed, not that it mattered now, as she'd probably blown it anyway. Rita caught the self pity look of her friend and quickly linked her arm through hers, urging her down the steps from the lynch gate and onto the gravel road.

'How about a nice piece of homemade apple pie and a coffee,' again catching Lisa's look, she added, 'no cinnamon in it I promise, it's a very English apple pie, not Canadian, so don't worry'; not that she had ever put spice in one even when living across the ocean.

The problem solved, the visitor forgotten, the three-some walked in companionship to number eleven, one of the row of small cottages facing the village green.

The wooden gate squeaked on its hinges and the small flower bush quivered as a marmalade-coloured cat hid itself in the foliage.

Once Rita had Lisa over the doorstep, she had no intention of letting her slip back into her self-imposed isolation and self-pity.

Lisa sat down on a kitchen chair, reluctant at first to shed her coat.

'How's the leg?' enquired Rita, while fiddling with a new coffee machine. She hadn't quite got the hang of it and Ernest had given up on it altogether.

'Fine.' Lisa's response was short and clipped; expressing the desire to end that topic of conversation.

'Good.' Rita responded and let the subject of Lisa's recovery from the gunshot wound drop. She clicked a switch on the new coffee maker, desperately hoping she had read the instructions on the leaflet correctly. She waited a second or two and when nothing alarming happened, she brought a couple of cups and saucers to the table, along with a large mug for her husband and some plates.

Lisa watched her friend lift a big apple pie out of her small fridge and place it in the microwave. Tension seemed to slip away from her shoulders; she felt safe and secure.

'So.' Rita had sat down and placed her elbows on the table; head cupped in her hands. 'What's happening now? Did they tell you how long you are to be suspended?'

Lisa coloured slightly and shifted her buttocks on the hard seat. A wisp of limp fair hair fell across her brow as she shrugged her shoulders.

Rita accepted the non-committal shrug, but pushed again for some response to her questioning. 'Heard from Jiten?'

Detective Constable Jiten Smith had worked along side Lisa when she was an acting the detective inspector on a case, which led to her suspension from the force over not calling for back-up in a difficult situation that ended with her boyfriend being convicted of homicide.

Jiten had been a pillar of strength for her a few times in their relationship with his philosophy on life and quiet manner.

Dark skinned, blue eyes, his father British and his mother Indian, he took the best from both of them; his father's practical mind and his mother's firm belief in Sankaya philosophy. Whenever he had tried to explain the philosophy to Lisa; she had not encouraged it.

'Pity,' Rita mused. She sliced a piece of pie onto a plate and pushed it forward, 'Ice cream?' Lisa shook her head, her mind flitting briefly back to Jiten's earlier talk on detachment, as though she had picked up on Rita's thoughts.

The door bell rang; breaking the silence that seemed to be developing. The two women looked at one another without moving. Lisa thought of Jiten, whilst Rita was visualising Frank Butterworth or even the unknown visitor once again standing at the door. They heard Ernest pad down the hallway from the front room, where he had been lighting the natural gas fire.

All ears were trained on the sound of the door opening and who it was. There was a murmuring of voices, a moment of suspense as the voices rose a little, then the door closing, then the sound of a visitor being led into the front room.

The two women looked at one another. Rita shrugged her shoulders. Lisa however looked animated and cautious. She leaned forward and, almost whispering. 'Do you think that chap's come back again?'

Rita nodded and giggled, although her curiosity aroused, she could not help making a joke. 'He won't get far if he's a salesman, Ernest eats them for breakfast.'

'On a Sunday?' Lisa exclaimed, looking a little surprised. Rita was amazed at her friend's thought pattern, whether it was the eating of a salesman on a Sunday, or the fact it was unlikely that salesmen would call on a Sunday. She shook her head. Slipping out of her chair and going to the kitchen door Rita opened it softly and listened carefully.

There was a murmur of voices before Ernest's voice rose; followed by the sound of arguing. Rita raised a thumb to Lisa, who joined her. The voices rose in volume, Ernest's becoming the loudest.

The two women looked at each other, a pin could have dropped in the stillness that followed, until Lisa whispered, 'I think the chap's come back, I really do.'

Rita's curiosity got the better of her as she widened the door opening. Holding up a hand to ward off Lisa, she whispered.

'Stay here luv, I'll just pop into the room and see what's going on.'

Lisa shrugged her shoulders reluctant to admit she felt rather put out. She sat down and stared at the pie before pulling it over towards her and reaching for the knife.

Meanwhile Rita stood by the closed front room door, her hand on the door-knob. Then taking a deep breath, she turned it and walked into the room. Both men were standing, and as they both turned at the interruption, Rita's heart raced and missed a few beats.

There was no denying the resemblance between the men, although the stranger was slightly smaller, with more weight and greyer in hair colour. But the eyes with the brooding eyebrows and the set of the mouth were identical. She smiled and thrust out her hand, now understanding that she was meeting for the first time a relative of her husband's, who for some reason had never once mentioned that he had any. 'You must be a relative of Ernest's.'

Rita smiled with delight and, as she was about to shake the firm hand grip, Ernest's voice chipped in.

'I don't have any relatives.' Ernest voice was tinged with sarcasm and anger as he stepped forward to protest. Still holding the strangers hand, Rita stared at her husband in confusion. The stranger pulled his own hand away, as if forgetting Rita's gesture and turned to Ernest.

'Believe me Ernest Heath, you do.' The man slid his hand into his pocket and pulled out a folded envelope. 'And I'm not just a distant relative,' he looked Ernest in the eye before adding; 'I am your brother.' He offered the stunned Ernest the envelope and continued, 'and here is the proof . . . .'

One could have heard a pin drop. Then, as an in-breath was sucked in, Rita readied herself for an explosion of words to follow. Ernest's face reddened, his jaw set as he gritted his teeth. Then all of a sudden he let out a long smooth breath, relaxing his shoulders and face muscles as his reasoning and logical mind took over.

He guessed the chap had got him mixed up, maybe there was some aunt or other he'd never known about, Ernest reasoned that was why even he could see some resemblance.

Well he could be gracious over mistakes and after all, they could be related; but a brother . . . . ? He almost laughed. That surely was pushing this ancestry business a bit too far. He leaned back as if he was now about to take some control of the situation.

Then a new thought emerged one that shook him to his core. He let the thought drift in the air, but both Ernest and Rita knew the answer well. It was an age when morality was paramount, and one sniff of scandal and one's life could be ruined. Ernest had gone a shade paler and all the steam now seemed to have gone out of him as he asked: 'If you are my brother; what happened. Why did nobody mention you?'

'Put into a home for adoption with lots like me.' The stranger stopped as he recalled his very early years, but then he suddenly brightened. 'Lucky though, my adoptive parents were the best; changed my name and gave me love, education and true family support.'

Rita broke in. 'So what is your name and what do you do?' He turned and studied her for awhile.

'Call me Roger . . . .' He paused before adding; 'I was a medical doctor. Retired now, and when my wife passed away, I lived in Canada with my daughter for a while.'

Again he stopped and looked down at his large hands. 'Missed the old country though, and needing to find my roots before I die.'

Ernest remained silent, his thoughts spinning. He felt a great anger, this person's childhood memories all probably a lie. Suddenly he heard Rita's voice again.

'Where are you staying?'

Roger shrugged his shoulders. 'Haven't looked around as yet, I just put first things first.' He glanced at Ernest who looked away. Rita caught it and wanted to smack her husband for his childishness and, without considering the consequences, added,

'Well that's settled Roger, you shall stay with us; we have a spare room.' A choke came from Ernest, and a sound of the front door closing.

Rita reddened in horror at her thoughtlessness. She'd forgotten all about Lisa.

Chapter 5

Lisa stood behind the closed front door of number seven, standing for a moment to regain her composure.

Her stomach was in knots and her shoulders tight, although her mind appeared to be stuck in no man's land, as if everything was switched to auto-pilot. The dark dreariness and silence of the passageway suddenly overwhelmed her and a long held in sound exploded from her mouth, followed by a cry of distress. Tears flowed freely down pale cheeks.

Not finding any means of wiping the flood-gates, she used her hands, feeling the wet surface spreading over her face. The small choking cries continued for a while before steadying and finally stopping altogether.

Lisa shook her head in an unconscious gesture of ending the self-pitying moment, but still aware of the tight knot of anxiety that refused to let go in her solar plexus.

Why had she just got up and left without any by-your-leave? God, she felt awful. That was no way to treat the two people she most respected in the whole world.

Lisa bit her lip to stop her self-pitying feelings. A long hard sniff helped and she pulled herself together and hung up her coat.

Entering the small kitchen with the idea of making herself a cup of tea only brought back the feeling of isolation. For a fleeting moment the smell of warm apple pie, coffee and other odours wafted through her memory, making sharp contrast to a kitchen before her of perfect order and cleanliness, but hardly lived in.

Even the computer on its small table in the corner of the room looked neglected and unused; in fact there was hardly any sign of anyone living there.

Lisa let her eyes roam around the room for a moment. She turned and quietly closed the door before opening the one on the right.

Nothing could be more opposite; the room was a mess, magazines lying abandoned on chairs, tables and the floor.

Plastic containers of convenience food and coffee mugs adding to the scene, some still filled with cold funny-coloured liquids.

Lisa made her way through the mess, sat on an old chair that had a crocheted shawl thrown over the back. She gazed at the fire's ash and cold part-burned coals, and thought of her mother. This time the tears flowed gently and the sobs increased.

'Mam where are you?' the words slipped out in a desperate attempt for some reunion. The church had brought the vision of her mother back so vividly. Not only sitting beside her wheel chair, occasionally bending over to turn the pages of her mother's hymnbook so she could follow the words. The church had meant a lot to her mam.

However the image was always replaced by the last time they had been together, and that was when Lisa had stood by the open grave.

Lisa leaned back in her mother's chair by the unlit fire and let the images drift by.

Robin; tall good-looking Robin, who had stirred her heartstring only to find out he was her cousin . . . . She let the feeling and the images sweep through her; then brought to focus the face of Ted.

The emotions that arose were mixed and fraught with anger. Ted the farmer, had brought her out of her self-pity, and she'd agreed to marry him; too late however for her to discover his dominating side and far worse, his twisted and sick mind.

Lisa closed her eyes and faced the horror that was always with her, especially at night.

Ted was a murderer, worst than that; a killer who had planned every move, even to their relationship.

Suddenly it sounded funny, and she wanted to laugh, the feeling rising hysterically and needing release.

Lisa squeezed her eyes tight and willed the feeling to go, thinking instead of her future. Her head dropped to one side and she bit her bottom lip as she analysed herself.

What sort of a person was she? Sighing she clung onto the thought process. Not very nice for one thing, as she'd just walked out of her friend's house without a by-your-leave.

Oh God, Lisa moaned to herself what have I done. Suddenly she just wanted to curl up in a foetal position and hide herself away from the world.

Ten minutes passed, she hadn't moved; her mind blank. Then the first seed of self preservation started to emerge and Lisa's inner strength stirred.

'What now?' she whispered to herself and the empty room. Years of analysing situations came to the surface; the bottom of the barrel had been reached. So what now?

Lisa opened her eyes; gazed at the ceiling and suddenly thought of Ernest. Why she didn't know? but it brought to mind her chosen profession.

'Did I really have a career in the police force?' Lisa mused. She faced the facts of her suspension and was no fool in thinking that her chances of making detective inspector would somehow be changed. Lisa knew she'd blown it for now in that direction, and who was to say she'd even get another chance.

Could she see herself staying as a detective sergeant all her working life? She thought of Jack Buzzard and how secretly he was seen as not quite having the smarts; especially after thirty years.

She shifted her position, sitting up straight. 'Better to get out of the police force altogether,' she muttered. 'Maybe even go to college and retrain for something else.'

For a while Lisa allowed herself to visualise other careers and possibilities, yet couldn't quite see herself doing anything else other than what she'd always wanted to do, that is to be in the police. She really couldn't be a nurse like Rita; looking after others needs all day long. She needed a challenge; something to get her head around, the excitement of the moment when that first call came in; the involvement and the interactions in pulling all the pieces together.

Lisa thought of Ernest. That's the sort of person she wanted to be like; always analysing the pieces of life's jigsaw, until the whole picture could be seen.

Suddenly the phone rang, which caused a moment of confusion as to whether it was the phone in the hall or the new cell phone she had acquired but was still getting used to. She listened again, this time convinced it was the phone in the hall, and for a fraction of a second remained where she was; almost ready to just let it keep ringing. However curiosity and regret got the better of her. She sighed; probably Rita wondering what the hell had happened to her.

She was right, it was Rita who, instead of asking her why she'd left without goodbyes, seemed to ignore that fact and proceeded to explain that the stranger was Ernest's brother, and wasn't that exciting.

'Very,' managed Lisa, the hint of sarcasm disregarded by her friend who chatted on about what a nice chap he was.

Lisa listened patiently, feeling more and more depressed at the realization that she wasn't so important in the Heath's life after all. She replaced the phone and had taken a couple of steps back, when it rang again. A soft voice came down the line.

'Lisa, its Jiten. Just calling to see how things are going.'

For one mad moment she wanted to shout back; how the hell do you think things are going? I'm suspended, using a bloody walking stick and living in an empty house with only myself to talk to.

She didn't of course and the conversation ended with her saying it was all okay if he wanted to call around; and to thank his mother for the card she'd sent and the home-baked biscuits.

'Dam,' she muttered. Banging her stick down heavily as she walked away from the phone. However a small part of her was relieved. If she was to have company, Jiten would be the one she could be honest with and there were no expectations on either side. He let her be totally herself; always.

Twenty minutes he'd said. Lisa hurried as fast as she could to try to create some order out of the room she'd neglected due to her own black moods.

So by the time Jiten's little car had parked out side and he'd entered number seven with a brown paper bag of home made scones his mother had made; Lisa had at least made some semblance of order around her.

Jiten was quick to notice the pinched flesh, devoid of make-up and the look he was greeted with. He had wanted to make contact with his old boss for some weeks and had always been forestalled.

So now, two feet over the threshold, he was going to use all his artillery on bringing the Lisa Pharies he knew back to life; aided by his mother's cooking initiatives.

'What's new?' Lisa faced the detective constable across the kitchen table, not willing to let the friendship develop to a cosy chat by the fire, unlit or not.

'One homicide;' he chewed slowly and swallowed the rather stale biscuit she'd placed before him rather than the offering he'd brought.

'Oh,' she said trying to look disinterested.

'A young girl; head bashed in, up on the Edge.' He sipped the weak coffee, adding 'I think the milk is slightly off. Got any fresh?' he asked.

'No,' Lisa shrugged, trying not to look too upset, but her mind was already visualizing the murder scene as she pulled more of the facts out of her former detective constable.

By the time the kitchen clock's big finger had circled the clock face twice, and the light fading outside; Lisa had extracted everything Jiten had to give; and when there was no more in the offing, she suggested it was getting late and he needed to be on his way.

Jiten rose, experiencing a slight discomfort; knowing full well he'd been put through both a washer and dryer on this one.

Lisa thanked him for coming and sent him on his way, but not before leaning a little forward at her open door to check if the car was still parked at number eleven. It was.

Chapter 6

Ernest didn't sleep a wink. It wasn't a matter of too much information to take in, neither excitement nor boredom, not even worry; the most common seeds of insomnia. All these conditions were but food for the daylight hours, not the time when the body needed rest.

Years of investigations into different problems that needed solutions had taught him that the night time hours were vital for resting the mind. He'd never had any trouble drifting off when his head hit the pillow.

Ernest wasn't even using his grey cells, in fact his whole body and mind seemed to be in a state of shock. Eyes wide open and body rigid, he stared into be black void around him. Even the movement on his chest of Rita's arm didn't clear away the void.

Occasionally the slight creak of the bed in the room attached to theirs could be heard, and once and only once Ernest's fingers curled; his nails biting into his palms.

The hours passed as they always had and would continue to do so. The blackness softening into grey and the occasional shadows appearing; before the first rays of morning sunlight stole through the crack in the partly open curtains, to send its stream across the room.

He didn't move, but watched the flickering of the sunlight; like a light bulb whose energy was fading and coming to its final end.

Thoughts and images of his mother's last days stole like a thief across his mind. She rocked gently in his gran's old chair; her legs covered with a worn tartan blanket.

What made the colours leap out he didn't know; but he saw the yellows, greens, reds and blacks so vividly. Her face in shadow, yet he knew its whiteness and thinness, the hollow cheeks and pale gaunt eyes . . . . Then the vision faded away to be replaced by a tall thin man with thick black eyebrows and eyes that demanded obedience.

Then the powerful body of his stepmother loomed; her large hands ready to take her frustration out on the small boy, who had grown so secretive and skilful at finding his own solutions to survival.

He couldn't see the boy; only feel him inside, the loneliness, the constant frustration and the ability of analysing situations.

A cold shiver passed through him, and he felt a warm body close the small gap between them. What if it was true and the reality of the situation he was faced with wasn't so bad after all, once he'd truly got used to the idea of having a brother.

Just quietly saying the word 'brother' to himself, kindled a strange feeling; he wasn't sure he could deal with it all. It wasn't just being presented with a sibling, but the knowledge of how little he really knew of his own parents.

He gave a fleeting sarcastic smile. He couldn't help thinking his new-found brother had done well, and had had opportunities much better than himself.

He turned his head and gazed at Rita. All at once telling himself that he was truly the lucky one. She turned, opened her eyes and smiled at him.

'Try to get a little sleep pet,' she said with a faint reproach, 'I'll get up and make us a nice cup of tea.'

He watched her get dressed, never quite overcoming the wonderment of how well she knew him. He hadn't been restless or talking in the night; so how the hell did she always know when he wasn't asleep.

He did drop off eventually, quite deeply in fact, only to be awakened a few minutes later . . . . , or so it seemed, by Rita standing over him with a tray of tea. He struggled up ready to take it and the newspaper under her arm, but she pulled back.

'Thought I'd take Roger the paper luv,' she said, giving a little laugh. 'No one's going to touch your puzzle, I promise.'

He let it go at that and sipped his tea, his mind now content to muse over the previous day's paper, and that one word that had foxed him in the crossword puzzle.

'Ah well,' he adjusted his position making sure he didn't spill any of the hot tea and contemplated the various places in town that he could recommend to Roger where one could stay for a few days.

Having settled on the Travellers Rest, he finished his tea and nestled back on his pillow before dropping into a deep sleep. He never heard their guest get up. Even the smell of eggs and bacon and the milkman's rattle of milk crates didn't disturb him.

When he did eventually open his eyes and looked at the watch on his wrist; it was well into the late morning and he noticed the curtains were still drawn.

He bit his bottom lip feeling a little guilty, while feeling the growing bristles on his chin. A good shower and a shave, something to fill the hole in his complaining stomach, and he'd feel as good as new.

Suddenly he realised the house sounded very quiet, not one murmur of voices. Dragging his dressing gown behind him, he went down the narrow flight of stairs to the kitchen door. Still no sound, and on opening it, was faced with an empty and very tidy kitchen; although the subtle smell of bacon still hung around.

The front room was also empty. He picked up yesterday's morning paper, tucked it underneath his arm and went back into the kitchen. Putting the kettle on, he flattened the newspaper and reached for a pencil.

His eyebrows came together in a frown of disbelief. He couldn't believe his own eyes for the crossword was almost completed.

He blinked, but there was no mistaking the word for the letters pencilled in were bold and straight, unlike his own. He tried to pronounce the word OCCIPITAL and focused on the clue given . . . . Part of the skull.

Looking again at the answer, he attempted to pronounce it to see if it rang a bell . . . . It didn't.

Honesty was one of Ernest's virtues, but he was having trouble accepting the fact that it was a word he wouldn't know. He would have never known the answer, even the other clue that hindered him filling in the letters, were again filled in with the same neat lettering; OPTIC.

The kettle boiled, but his thirst had diminished, never before had anyone touched his crossword, even if he didn't complete it. He knew who had done it, and felt suddenly defiled and humiliated.

His appetite for food lessened, his main concern now being where the hell was Rita. He phoned Lisa, muttering about needing to ask his wife something; then felt more of a fool when she told him she wasn't there.

Two hours later and experiencing a changing mood from annoyance to anxiety, the front door opened. Rita laughed at something. He heard Roger's chuckle as they came in and flopped down in chairs; looking at him.

'Ernest, we had a lovely lunch, you should try the little new café on Spring Street. They do the best soup.' Rita smiled at her companion. 'Great wasn't it?'

Roger grinned back. 'I tried to persuade Rita to drive my car, but she wasn't having any of it; said it had far too many new-fangled gadgets in it.'

Ernest gave a half glimpse of a smile, and tried to appear accommodating.

'Roger, I've been thinking. If you are planning on staying for a few days, I could take you to the Travellers Rest.'

There was a sharp intake of breath from Rita.

'Don't be silly luv; Roger is family. He stays here.' She paused, and looking at Roger added; 'for as long as he likes.' The new-found family member patted her hand, smiling and showing a perfect set of natural teeth in the process.

'I'd love to stay awhile. There are a few things I've got planned.' He paused and lingered over his next words. 'I feel I belong here,' while looking Ernest straight in the eye. 'I do need to do a few things like seeing my real parent's graves and their old home.'

'God forbid.' Ernest murmured to himself; 'reality and imagination so very much apart,' he thought. He was just about to make some sarcastic remark, when Rita jumped in again.

'Ernest, you know what,' she giggled like a school girl. 'Roger actually spent a year at the Toronto Hospital.'

'This is all I need,' moaned her husband to himself; the two of them talking about the land of milk and honey, cold winters, pizzas and hamburgers. His misery hadn't yet ended as Roger glanced at the newspaper.

'Good crossword in today's old boy. I've already done half of it.' He looked across at Rita. 'Did it in bed; thanks Rita for bringing it up this morning.'

Rita had the grace to flush a little as she caught Ernest eye. She got up quickly, and opened the fridge door.

'What do you want to eat luv?' she said staring at the inside of it with very little enthusiasm.

Ernest coughed. The day wasn't starting off all that well. 'I'm alright; maybe I'll just wander up to the Horseshoe later.' He regretted his words right away.

'Lovely, I'll come with you, Rita will be glad of a rest from us men-folk for a while.'

Rita shuffled up to the kitchen sink, trying to look busy. Ernest's neck was already going red.

Chapter 7

'Everyone here;' It was voiced more as a command than a question. Detective Superintendant Wigfull swept into the room, he surveyed the area, and then frowned slightly as the door opened and someone entered backwards holding a plastic cup in each hand.

Sergeant Jack Buzzard's placid face never flinched as he handed a hot coffee to a young fresh looking constable leaning by the wall.

A slight sigh came from the superintendent before turning his attention to the main body of attentive men and women, some in uniform others in a variety of plain clothes from collar and tie to jeans and T-shirts. The latter group having just arrived off the streets; where they had been mingling with the locals in a conscious attempt to pick up any vital bits of information.

The detective superintendant cleared his throat, and then turned his back on his waiting audience. Folding into a roll the half-folded newspaper he was carrying; he tapped on the board with it against the name Anna Booth.

His voice rose suddenly as he read it out loud. Dozens of pairs of eyes flashed from the written word to the speaker. He repeated the name, as if to make certain it was never forgotten. A sensitive soul would have picked up sadness as it was spoken.

The detective superintendant went on; his tone now formalized into imparting information.

Anna Booth; aged ten years.

* The body discovered by a hiker on Saturday, 11 March, 1996 at 11.55 a.m. on the Edge; the location not far from her home on Edge Road.
* The body found lying at the foot of a standing stone, known as the Maidenstone.
* The skull crushed; assumed to have been caused by a heavy blow to the head.
* A rock found nearby and covered in blood; thought to be the murder weapon.

There was silence, as the detective superintendant surveyed the attentive audience for any input he might get from the various teams. Nothing was forthcoming; they knew from experience he hadn't finished imparting information, and didn't like to be interrupted.

'We are still awaiting the time of death and the autopsy report, before we can proceed fully. The parents have been informed. They weren't aware she had gone on the Edge apart from the fact that she was writing an essay for her school on the origins of the Bronze Age Maidenstone.'

A hand went up. The detective superintendant looked surprised at being interrupted, but nodded to the officer to state whatever he had to say.

'Sir, the Maidenstone is Neolithic, not Bronze Age.'

Someone twittered, the detective superintendant's face flushed, but years of experience came into play and instead of making some sarcastic remark, he thanked the officer for being observant in the details.

Someone else's whispered voice was barely heard as he spoke, and only to his closest companions.

'Anna Booth went to the same school as the super did as a boy.

'Was he ever a boy?' The comment created a ripple of amusement as it swept on like a gentle wave across the room. The superintendant tapped his side with the rolled paper and looked over towards a slim, under-weight man who had been quietly standing to the right of him.

'Detective Chief Inspector Granger here will be heading up the investigation, I expect full time given to the smallest detail; no stone unturned and the case resolved as soon as possible.' The detective superintendant spoke slowly and; as if determined to stamp his overall authority on the case, added: 'No vacations, and any leave underway cancelled. Do I make myself clear?'

There was a murmur of acceptance, and the detective superintendant nodded back to them all.

Detective Chief Inspector Granger stepped forward, his slight countenance and pale skin didn't lend itself to the same command of the situation as his superior. However his sharp intelligence far out-weighed first appearances. Nothing ever missed his attention, as others had quickly found out, much to their regret.

Another wave of murmuring again petered out, only to leave the occasional sound of a throat-clearing and a shuffling of feet to help the blood circulation.

Detective Chief Inspector Granger picked up a folder that lay on the table by the end wall. He opened it, taking out an enlarged black and white photo, which he swiftly pinned onto a cork-board behind him. He repeated the super's opening words.

'Anna Booth.'

Someone moaned; the hole in the side of the skull clearly visible on the photograph. The detective inspector ignored it and proceeded to reiterate the facts already given by his superior, although this time he began at the first reporting of the body.

'Buzzard.' His steely blue eyes locked onto the desk sergeant. 'You first received the call at . . . , he waited.

'Saturday morning sir.' The police sergeant stood taller as he became aware of all the attention around him.

'Time man, Saturday, 11 March at . . . ?' He waited.

Buzzard took out his note book: reading out the precise hour and minutes . . . , someone giggled.

A large detailed map of the area had been unfolded and pinned up on another board beside the photo of the victim. It showed the gentle slope at the end of the Pennine range, with dotted marks indicating walking paths. Over to the left; a wider road with a number of small squares representing cottages.

Halfway on the side of the sloping land, darker shapes were identified by a red marker; one by a half circle and further to the east, another solitary one circled fully.

Most members of the town's police force knew personally, or from the history of the town, what these areas represented. Few had actually visited them, but like everything in the UK; it was taken for granted the past would always be around them.

The larger of the darker areas indicated the site of a long cairn; a Bronze Age burial mound made of stone which once covered burial chambers.

The second circle contained only one stone, thought to have been erected by the first small band of Neolithic people for sacrificial purposes.

'This is the area on which we will concentrate.' The inspector narrowed his eyes, the almost white lashes making only thin slits visible.

'We want to know if there are any established walking groups who use these paths, any curious sight-seer's asking about the burial chamber and anyone who knows anyone else who regularly walks around that area; photographers, birdwatchers, wild-life enthusiasts, and . . . , anyone who'd been there for a spot of courting.' At the last remark, a faint tinge of red coloured his cheeks. He turned away and faced the map again.

'Check how many ways there are to get to the paths from the road. Talk to people who own the cottages, and . . . , talk to the murdered girl's friends again and any other that might know her. Has she been seen with anyone lately; stranger or not?'

He looked around, waiting for anything else or anybody to voice an opinion. Groups had now formed and the room by this time was buzzing.

As certain members of the scene-of-crime team gave their account, a clearer picture was beginning to emerge; from the prevailing weather conditions at the time of the murder to the first finding of the body, and the later forensic investigation information.

Outside it had begun to rain, quietly at first then with a heavier drumming on the window panes, the noise accompanied by the sharp tapping on a computer keyboard, where everything was being recorded.

Police Sergeant Jack Buzzard moved out of the way as everyone now seemed to be heading towards the door. Someone knocked his arm, splashing coffee over the cuff of his white shirt. He looked at it for a second, then pulled the sleeve of his jacket over it; his thoughts far from having to deal with any stains.

There had been a moment during the presentations he'd wanted to stop the detective chief inspector and tell the whole assembly something was amiss. He reckoned this was a copy-cat murder; a murder very similar to one that had happened many years before. Back then there were little forensics, certainly no computers or modern gadgets; just their investigative skills and their own intelligence to call on.

He let out a deep breath, which those near him thought was due to tiredness; him now being ready for retirement and an arm-chair; instead of having to stand for long hours.

However his exhale was really an admittance of a past failure, the only failure in a team he'd once been part of as a detective constable; a team that his idol, Ernest Heath was part of all those years before.

As for the crime scenes; he'd seen them all over again today as clear as crystal. A young girl, lying stretched out with her hands folded across her chest and a little bunch of wild flowers under them. It was the head, or what was left of it, that had made him vomit then. Parts of the brain mixed with fragments of bone and blood. Being sick at the crime scene had not gone too well with the powers that be and when he asked to come off the case and return to being a desk constable, no-one stood in his way.

That sight of the young girl's body lying at the foot of the Maidenstone had clearly unhinged him all those years before.

He'd tried to get the words out just now; to remind the superintendant that new case seemed to be a copy-cat case of one thirty years earlier, but his body and voice had frozen during the meeting.

The room now was almost empty; the super gone, and the inspector was packing up some of the remaining paper work.

Sergeant Buzzard took a deep breath and closed the distance between them. Once there, he inhaled again and the words tumbled out.

'Sir, I believe this is a copy-cat murder; same murder weapon and a young girl involved.'

Detective Chief Inspector Grainger stared at him; not sure whether the police sergeant had taken a turn for the worse. He'd always suspected there being something different about him, but couldn't quite pin it down.

'Thirty years ago there was a case identical to this one; young girl, head bashed in and left at the base of the same stone on the Edge.' He paused before sucking in a lungful of air, as more words were about to spill out. The DI's eyes opened in surprise; then narrowed, as he took stock of the man in front of him.

'Go on sergeant.' The detective chief inspector arched his buttocks up and sat on the end of the table.

'I was a young detective constable at the time,' informed Buzzard. Surprise flicked over the chief's face for a second.

'Heath was on the team.' Buzzard waited . . . , expecting some acknowledgement of the name, but none was forthcoming. 'Detective Inspector Heath.' Buzzard now was in full swing. 'He retired not so long ago, lives in Gelsby, got re-married and . . . .' The detective chief inspector held up his hand.

'Oh . . . . Him.'

Not only did the conversation last for most of the rest of the day, but the coming-up-for-retirement sergeant was given a comfortable chair in the chief inspector's office and was plied with more coffee than usual that perked him up to thinking this was turning out to be the best day of his life.

Eyes followed the upright figure as he eventually closed the door of the detective chief inspector's room behind him. He smiled benevolently at everyone and put on his overcoat for home.

He would have felt quite upset if he'd heard the murmurings he'd left behind him. The talk among them being that maybe he had just been asked to retire now and not in a few weeks time.

Chapter 8

Rita had taken Roger for a walk around the village, letting him encourage her into taking a daily constitutional that Ernest had not thought necessary.

'Good for the old legs,' remarked Roger; bending his knees and stretching his leg muscles a few times.

'With all the walking I've done in my time, I think the old legs could do with a rest.' Ernest retorted; leaving them feeling he was just being funny. Rita sighed and went to fetch Roger's coat.

Roger adjusted his tie in front of the mirror, blocking Ernest's view of the fireplace. Ernest felt his nerves coiling into tight springs, but waited patiently for the front door being closed behind them before flopping into his favourite chair and staring at the ceiling.

It didn't last long before he sat upright; his fingers tapping on the arms of the leather chair. He glanced at the newspaper; grinding his teeth together and tapping even harder.

Suddenly like a vulture in flight he swooped forward and snatched up the paper, his mind refusing to acknowledge that anyone could do the extra hard crossword that quick. His gloomy mood lessened as he contemplated sarcastically into finding mistakes.

Reaching over for his well bitten pencil that lay with a few others under his chair, he opened the paper at the sports page; obviously the paper having been used and not re-assembled to its original page numbering, which again brought on a feeling of annoyance. Faced now with the front page, he stared at it, stunned by what he read.

The headlines leapt out.

Local Girl's Body Found on the Edge.

There was a small photograph of the victim to one side, he glanced at the face, young, fresh, full of life, before reading on.

Anna Booth aged 10, only daughter of Philip and Jane Booth was discovered by a hiker on Saturday. Her body was lying by the well-known Maidenstone on the Edge. Foul play is suspected, and the police are asking anyone who saw her that morning or have any other information to contact them at once.

Ernest read on mechanically, stopping briefly at certain words. The word Maidenstone leapt out, and his whole body went cold; before starting to shake.

The past leapt forward like an animal that had been locked away for years; its claws gripping at his chest, causing shallow breathing.

Suddenly anger erupted, it hit hard; the feeling not coming from the knowledge of the young girl's death, but from his own failure.

His first investigation as a young dedicated detective came to mind. He had been totally committed, proud of his skills with the view of rising rapidly in his chosen career. Then it came to a stop, not for ever but what seemed to him at the time as a lifetime.

He'd made a mistake.

'Ye Gods, has it all broken loose again in my life,' he muttered. First a stranger presents himself out of the blue, and now a copy-cat murder that he'd tried so hard to push out of his mind as one that had got way, although never forgotten. Deep down he still believed he was right in his suspicion and it still angered him that it had never been investigated further.

He folded the paper in the correct order, slid his fingers down the fold and folded it again: tucking it under his arm as he got up. He knew exactly where he was going as he opened the front door.

The air was cold; the cold dampness after the rain. His old cardigan lacked the warmth of wool; being synthetic. The ground still wet in places dampened his tartan slippers as he padded his way to number seven.

He stood, his finger pressed against the bell, until the door flung open and a flushed angry face appeared, ready to give the bell pusher a mouthful.

Seeing Ernest, she stood aside, quickly assessing his wearing attire and the dark look on his face. She'd seen it all before and knew well to keep quiet until the storm broke. He marched into the kitchen without saying a word, took the newspaper from under his arm and placed it on the table. He stared at her before demanding;

'Have you seen this?'

Lisa felt little shell-shocked; as all manner of situations flitted through her mind.

Had she said or done something; she couldn't think properly. After all, she hadn't been around or talked to anyone really for over three months. Yet her stomach was full of butterflies, recalling the reason why she had been suspended. She wondered what had come up and stared at him.

'Here.' He opened the folded newspaper showing the headlines. Lisa stared down at it, trying to concentrate on the writing and Ernest's voice at the same time. 'Another young girl, same place, same age, and I bet she was killed in the same way.' There was a hint of hysteria growing.

'Ok Ernest, simmer down and let me read this.' She said; pointing to the article and pulling up a chair.

Ernest acknowledged her sensibility with a sigh and a nod of his head, joining her; scraping his chair legs along the tiled floor and causing Lisa to grit her teeth.

After a few minutes she looked up at his face; his eyes now staring into hers.

'Terrible Ernest, poor little soul, her parents must be devastated . . . ,' she was about to continue, but was interrupted by a blast of emotion.

'You don't understand and how could you? You were only a child at the time.'

Lisa could only sit and stare at him; not knowing what to say or where this was all leading, but over the years she'd worked for him, she knew only too well to pin back her ears and listen. 'Go on, Gov.,' the old title slipping out with habit.

Ernest arched his back and rolled his neck, before leaning forward and spreading his large hands in front of him.

'Thirty years ago I' . . . , Lisa did a quick sum and muttered 1966. Ernest stared at her for a minute, and then nodded. 'Okay, in 1966, I had great expectations of a higher rank in the offing.'

Lisa raised her eyebrows, not quite knowing whether it was actually on the cards or just plain vanity. A weak smile followed as Ernest started to explain.

'I was ambitious; I had found something I was good at. I was a great believer in justice and had worked hard. Oh, it was on the cards alright; paper work done, hints here and there.'

'So?' Lisa wondered what had happened since then that had delayed his advancement all those years before, as he was only a detective inspector when she was assigned to his team later.

'That expected promotion? Well it didn't happen then; not for many years after.'

'Why on earth not?' asked Lisa. It seemed unbelievable that it had taken so long, and secretly she'd often wondered why he'd never got to be a chief detective inspector; for his reputation for solving crimes was well known.

By now he had calmed down; as he came to terms with the cause of his nemesis. He was ready to state only the facts clearly; without personal injections and feelings.

'As I said before, in 1966 I was part of a homicide that was delicate, because the murdered girl was young and local, and as you can imagine, feelings in Danesbury were rife. Fear paramount for parents with young children at having a killer lose. Suspicions were readily aroused at anyone not quite conforming to the image of an upright citizen.'

'I can see that,' murmured Lisa, knowing only too well how small towns react. 'Go on.'

'I remember it was June time.' He stopped momentarily before stating 'June 6th, a group of hikers were climbing up to the Edge to get a better view of the area, on coming down they noticed a flock of crows.'

'A murder of crows,' interrupted Lisa, but on seeing the blank look, she added, 'a flock of crows is known as a murder of crows.' She quickly regretted her interruption.

Ernest merely shook his head, and continued; 'as they wandered down, someone pointed out that they were walking towards an old Neolithic monument. There they found her; the girl with her head bashed in. She'd been laid out; arms crossed her chest with a bunch of wild flowers under one hand.'

Ernest's voice choked a little, at the memory. It was the first time he'd ever seen the body of a child; either by a natural death or following a homicide.

'Golly that must have been hard to take.'

'More so for Jack Buzzard,' replied Ernest, noting Lisa's eyebrows lifting. 'Yes he and I joined the force together and both of us were in the investigation branch.' Lisa came to realise how little she really knew of the officers she'd worked with.

'Buzzard couldn't take it, a little soft is our Jack,' added Ernest.

Lisa understood; Jack's emotions and sympathetic nature had often got the better of him.

'He asked to go back to being a constable and spent most of his time on the desk, he was happy with his lot, mind.'

'And you?' Lisa still didn't know what had happened that had so affected her old gov's career.

'Me?' Ernest gazed for a moment at the paper, before adding, 'I arrested an innocent person.'

Now his confidant's back straightened and she looked at him with wide eyes.

'Beat him up before arresting him.' Ernest was now wrestling with his past.

Lisa sighed, 'and you say he was proved innocent.'

'Aye.'

'What happened, and who was it.'

'I arrested the girl's father.' His voice seemed to slip away, the room became silent. 'He was supposed to be at work, but we found out he had skived off . . . , fishing.'

'So it wasn't him . . . . ,' remembering he'd said he'd arrested the wrong person.

'Seemed not; a friend came forward and gave him an alibi.'

'Someone close?' Lisa had really no idea why she'd asked that question. A slip of a smile hovered at the end of Ernest's mouth.

'Oh yes, real close; a brother in fact, who happened to be my superior, the detective chief inspector.'

'Ah,' was the only sound forthcoming.

'Dead now,' Ernest explained, as if there wasn't any more to be done with that evidence.

'Who?'

'Both the detective chief inspector and the girl's father; the father committed suicide after finding he'd got cancer.'

In a moment of deep affection for the man she saw as a father figure and her much revered superior in her job, she leaned forward and clasped his hand.

'And an identical homicide has happened again after thirty years . . . , copy-cat by all accounts,' she added.

Her old gov. didn't comment; he just shrugged his shoulders, looked at her for a moment before asking,

'Isn't it time you asked that nice young detective constable around . . . ? Smith isn't it.'

'Yes Ernest, you know quite well his name, and yes I will give Detective Constable Jiten Smith a call.

She saw where he was going and was surprised at the leap of excitement in her stomach. She chuckled; it was a good emotional feeling, and Ernest felt better too. There was something about puzzles that perked him up, even if they were old ones.

Chapter 9

The house was quiet when Rita and Ernest's brother returned from their walk. Rita noticed it right away, making her feel more guilty than she already was.

Guilty in part for leaving her husband looking dejected by the fire, she knew how his puzzles had become a vital part of his daily routine; something to focus on and exercise his skills in clue hunting. She also felt bad about the walk being longer than planned as Roger had insisted he buy her lunch at the Horseshoe.

The latter she hadn't enjoyed one bit, as the locals were obviously speculating on the new man in her life. At one point she was almost ready to stand up and introduce her husband's brother, but had reminded herself that if they looked long and hard enough, they could see the resemblance for themselves. She had tried to blot out the wink and nod towards her companion by the barman, and she had been determined not to give him the satisfaction of knowing who Roger was.

All the time she had been eating the well prepared lobster salad, and sipping wine, Ernest's face had kept appearing. Funny, she reminded herself, it was always the face of the little boy she saw and not the man's, when she thought she was neglecting him.

Looking at her watch and checking the time on the brass-faced clock on the black beam over the fire surround, she reckoned it was time to go home.

Her heart had given a few fast beats and she knew she was getting anxious. Roger seemed to sense her restlessness and made no objection when she drank the last of her white wine, stood up and slipped on her coat.

True to form he was behind her in an instant lifting it over her shoulders. For some odd reason she wished he wasn't such a gentleman, for it was far harder for her to give him less attention in return. However Ernest needed his lunch, and he always came first. Any idea that he was capable of getting his own would have unsettled her motherly instincts towards him.

When they did arrive home, it was a great surprise to find her husband biting into a large beef sandwich, the roast still sitting on the table with a knife by it at the ready for more. Quickly she calculated the amount needed later and automatically lifted the dish up and placed it in the fridge. Ernest looked up from the paper and smiled.

'Good walk?' It was a question that lacked interest.

'Had lunch at the pub,' chipped in Roger, slipping the kettle on and reaching for the cups.

Rita coloured and turned to the cutlery drawer, and stood stiff for a moment not quite believing her husband's response.

'Good food that place serves, you should get Rita to take you on a Friday; the fish and chips are to die for, not to mention the mushy peas.'

Even Roger was a little taken aback at Ernest's change in attitude and glanced at Rita who kept her back turned.

'Sorry about the crossword old man,' chirped in Roger trying to find a complete acceptance of their relationship.

'Think nothing of it.' Again Rita began to wonder if Ernest was having a breakdown, or building up to a bombshell; like telling their visitor it was time he went.

But nothing occurred to rock the boat, and at one point Rita could have sworn she heard Ernest humming.

The day passed as it must, and the evening shadows closed in. Ernest lit the fire, Rita turned on the TV, and Roger found the local paper minus the front page and to his slight annoyance, the cross-word done.

Rita picked up a sweater she'd started to knit months before, and it never seemed to grow, the truth being she really didn't like knitting but it passed the time away on those really boring evenings when her husband had his head behind the newspaper.

The BBC news came on and she put her needles down, but was suddenly confronted with Ernest's back as he leaned over and changed the channel.

'You like nature shows don't you pet.' The next thing she was looking down the mouth of a huge grizzly that the camera man had zoomed in on.

She sensed Roger looking at her, and started to knit faster. It had become a confusing day; the man she knew better than anyone, seemed to be changing as the hours passed. His cheerfulness, his acceptance of his hardly known brother especially letting him do his puzzles and now changing over from the only TV programme he watched regularly. She glanced over at him and noticed a constant flick of his head, as if he was listening out for the phone or the door bell to ring.

She gazed at him over her reading glasses and decided there and then; he was up to something. Some things don't change and these give-away signs hadn't failed her as a girl and remained with her as a woman. One thing was for certain, Rita knew Ernest better than any-one and he was up to something; of that she had no doubt at all.

She got up to make coffee, the nature film boring her. Ernest smiled as she passed and touched her hand in affection. She frowned, still a little confused.

The phone rang, Ernest leapt up and she had to step quickly aside as he made for the hall. Loitering a little by the kitchen door, she allowed her sense of hearing to adjust.

'Lisa; did he . . . ,' there was a pause. 'Good, good, yes I'll pop around, and look surprised for goodness sake; we don't want him feeling cornered.'

There was a silence as Ernest listened to the speaker, then; 'no it's not a problem; they're watching TV.' Then a pause . . . , 'did you watch it? What did they say?

Again silence as Ernest gave the speaker his full concentration. 'Two minutes, good,' he put the phone down, turned and saw his wife looking at him.

He bit his bottom lip. A sign Rita had seen many times during their school years. He was up to something.

'Lisa needs some help pet,' he said pulling on his old anorak. 'Don't know how long it will take, but best just pop my dinner in the oven.'

'Ernest;' Rita's voice was low, edged with a warning sound of frustration, but it was all to no avail as he closed the front door behind him.

He recognised Jiten Smith's small black car parked too close to the pavement as usual, wondering how many more times the detective constable needed a warning, before he was forced to change his tires, as all the outside tyre walls were badly scraped.

The cat that seemed to think the middle of Lisa's small garden path was made for sleeping; stirred and fled.

Lisa welcomed him, she looked better than she had for a long time; and Ernest even thought it would be in order to use the word pretty.

She'd obviously washed her hair, and whether the dryness of the overly warm house or a cosmetic aid, the limpness had gone giving it body. He also detected a touch of lipstick and the eyebrows and eyes more defined and darker.

She generally wore a T-shirt and jeans which seemed to be her usual off-duty uniform; but the red top she was now wearing suited her, and the jeans were not the patched ones she once seemed to favour, although they were just as faded.

Jiten had made himself at home beside a well-banked-up fire. Lisa had brought out three bottles of pale ale, and a plate of rather flat hard-looking home made biscuits, which Jiten was already biting on with his strong white teeth. 'Great baking Lisa,' he remarked.

Lisa blushed and gave a little cough. Ernest looked at him in amazement, and declined an offering; murmuring it would spoil his dinner. Jiten's hand stretched out for another before he sat back contentedly; not saying another word.

Ernest and Lisa looked at one another; before she shrugged her shoulders; indicating what the hell was there to lose.

'You must be busy Jiten.' Lisa used his first name claiming intimacy. 'Just read the papers about the girl found on the Edge.' Ernest pretended to be far more interested in the length of his own finger nails.

'God, yes, the whole department's gone mad.' Jiten sighed, indicating he was very much involved, 'Even thought they might cancel my day off.'

'Any clues?' Ernest asked, as if it was just polite conversation and noted, rightly so; the young detective constable was animated by the interest of his peers.

'Any info. coming from the house-to-house enquires?' asked Ernest. Jiten shrugged his shoulders, before adding; 'no boy friends as far as we know.'

Ernest couldn't help himself . . . , 'boy friends at her age?' Lisa gave him one of her looks and he sat back.

'Anyone in the picture?' she asked innocently, she offered Jiten another biscuit, and he took it smiling. 'No.' he stated flatly to the question.

'Not a pretty sight, I reckon.' Ernest just couldn't help himself.

Jiten considered his question, a feeling of being under pressure had built up and he responded automatically. 'Horrible; all crunched up, as though she was trying to defend herself before being bashed on the head.'

Ernest was quick to note that only the police would know that. Nothing had been said in the papers, he felt almost guilty in pressing the likeable lad.

'Maybe her next life will be better.' Jiten offered. Ernest and Lisa stared at him in amazement at his remark.

'So Jiten; no one in the frame, as we would say,' asked Lisa.

Jiten shook his head and helped himself to the lone remaining biscuit on the plate. Lisa got up to fetch some more and make coffee, and by the time she'd returned, Ernest had got the names of the whole investigation team, the details of what was known and the fact that Sergeant Buzzard had spent a long time with the detective chief inspector; although his retirement was not for another six weeks.

Ernest half smiled; the lad doesn't miss much.

Jiten left later, he got in his car, feeling a little discomfort in his stomach. Indigestion he decided, never thinking of another possible cause. He did feel however as if his mind had been spring-cleaned, but happily set off home scraping his tyres on the curb as he did so.

Ernest was late home for his dinner which he never-the-less warmed up and ate with relish. He snored contentedly all night by Rita's ear and even offered to get up and make a pot of tea in the morning.

To Rita it had been a day of surprises. To Ernest and Lisa; a day of entering again the world they loved best.

Chapter 10

Ernest's good mood didn't last long, for as he lay staring into the darkness again that night. It hit him that he was of no value to any investigation.

Outsider to knowledge, the in-depth knowledge, not just the tit-bits gleaned from the local rag and from the good-natured D.C Smith. He was the outsider to the involvement of any investigation now.

The reality hit him hard, his body felt cold even with Rita's warmth nestled beside him. A guilt feeling arose too. He'd seen Lisa's face light up and her eyes shine like they used to.

Suddenly Ernest felt a spent force and a fraud. He wasn't in the investigation game anymore. He didn't have a team of enthusiastic people around him. There wasn't any clues to follow up on; nothing to solve.

He suddenly wanted to laugh. Of course there were his puzzles, hours of placing letters and numbers in little boxes. That's what his world was now wrapped around.

The darkness closed in; around and inside his body. The feeling of depression hung about, awaiting the final door to open and take over.

Rita stirred and sighed.

Ernest cursed himself and stretched his neck over the edge of the pillow; pulled up the blankets and turned sideways towards the warm body. He slipped his arm across Rita's waist and inched himself towards her so that they lay like a couple of spoons; interlocked.

A slight scent of lavender hung in the air. It was pleasant and filled with past memories. He made a silent vow to let go of the past and who he once was, and concentrate on his and Rita's future together.

A momentary ghost of Roger slipped through defences only to be dealt with positively. A quick trip up to the church to visit their parent's grave, maybe a stop off to show his brother the old two-bedroomed terraced house, now marked for demolition; it being part of the site for a new mall.

He was beginning to feel hospitable and better. He liked the new feeling; planning a trip to Rudyard with lunch on him before waving Roger off. He stopped short his mental process from ending with . . . , for good. There were bound to be Christmas cards and the occasional phone call. Most families close or not did that; he recalled, although in truth he'd had little experience. For that matter; he'd never sent or even bought a Christmas card, but Rita . . . . He fell asleep; not even disturbed by the thunder that rolled in waves through the early morning skies.

The God Thor was in good mettle, for the thunder and lightening continued most of the morning, bringing with it dark clouds that threatened more downpours of rain.

It was 11.30 am before the phone rang, as Ernest was showing his brother the few photos he possessed of his family. Their mother and father at some wedding, black and white and cracked at the corners; where they had once been held by some corner stickers in an album. One of their gran, caught off guard; her hair in curlers and a turban wrapped around them.

Ernest looked closer at the wrap-around apron she wore, and wondered if she had other clothes to wear underneath, as he couldn't remember her wearing anything else.

The phone rang again, nobody moved; and Rita's hands covered in flour from her baking. They looked at each other before Ernest lifted himself out of his chair with a sigh.

'Alright, alright.' He raised his hands in surrender and left the room.

Rita carried on kneading the dough, and Roger continued to look at the old black and white photos, trying hard to find some resemblance of himself; while ignoring the feeling of being somewhat thankful he had been brought up by his adopted parents. But as his analyst had said, it was better to come to terms with one's past rather than live in make-believe land.

It was exactly that same feeling that swept through Ernest as he put down the phone. His first reaction was similar to someone hearing that they had won a lottery.

Disbelief, then every nerve cell stimulated; the world now full of endless possibilities. The powers that be wanted Ernest to head up a cold case team.

His Achilles' heel; the only case he was unable to solve; and neither had anyone else for that matter.

He took in a deep breath, looked at the phone he was still holding, the peeping signal telling him to hang up.

He replaced it slowly, his hand sliding downward, as if caressing it.

Ernest stepped back but instead of re-entering the kitchen, he sat on the bottom step of the stairs, staring into space; the words of the chief detective inspector still ringing as clear as crystal in his ears.

'It's been authorised from the top Heath, you pick your own team and space will be made, with all the assistance you need.'

Right away he'd known the people he could work with and trust to be totally committed, and he considered his options quickly. PC Buzzard, not because of any investigative skills he might have, but for the very fact he was there in 1966 and part of that homicide team.

Ernest left his first choice to the last, afraid of a refusal concerning more recent past events. Of course if the need was great, ways could always be found, and it sounded like the need was indeed great.

Detective Sergeant Pharies was his choice, and he was determined to stick out for it, although he hadn't said as much over the phone when accepting the time and place for a confidential talk with the powers that be.

He had confirmed he would be at the Danesbury Police Headquarters that afternoon at 3.00 pm, knowing too well he would have to cancel the dentist's appointment Rita had made for him. Slipping his tongue into the small hole where the filling had dropped out, he decided it could wait.

Rita turned as he came back into the kitchen, noting the flush on his face and wondering if he should up his blood pressure tablets.

'Who was it luv?' she asked with a disinterested voice, it was Monday and everyone she knew would be busy after the weekend, even if only cleaning the house or starting back to work again. The only person she had in mind as a possibility was Frank Butterworth with some local gossip.

Ernest leaned against the doorway wall. He felt suddenly years younger. Better to tell the truth and be done with it, because he already knew the path he'd chosen.

He stood up straight. 'That my love was the chief inspector of the homicide division, and . . .' He let it hang awhile, noting the two faces that had all his attention. 'He's asked me to head up a cold case team.'

He waited for the reaction. Roger just sat and stared not quite understanding, and Rita carried on doing what she had been doing.

Silence followed.

'Great luv,' she said. 'It will give you something to do.'

Ernest stared at his wife; he felt she owed him more than that. What about surprise, objection even; but not just a good-for-you, old boy.

He looked at Roger who in turn looked at him with a similar vacant expression. 'I'll be out a lot, but paid.' It sounded feeble and childish.

Rita shrugged. 'Good for you dear, when do you start?' As always his wife's remarks took the wind out of his sails and brought him down to reality.

'Got a meeting this afternoon at 3.00 pm. It's about a case I once investigated that was never resolved.' He looked up sheepishly. 'Thought I'd try to involve our Lisa.

Rita looked unfazed. 'Great; there you go then, see how everything works out. Do you both good.' she added.

Roger still hadn't said a word, his eyes moving from one to the other, the intimacy of the two beyond him.

Ernest sighed, he'd got it all; the only love of his life, retirement and no worries. He was feeling the old excitement rising; his thoughts already on past events and memories stirring and coming into the present.

The time past slowly, he checked his watch frequently to the amusement of his wife. Adrenaline began flowing through his veins as the hours passed. The clouds at one point becoming very dark, releasing another downpour of rain that thrashed against the windows, and pebbled on the roof with sharp sounds.

Then it stopped, the dark clouds faded and lost form as the sun appeared; tentatively at first, before growing bolder and brighter.

The clock, with species of painted birds instead of numbers; clicked rhythmically in the kitchen until it reached two-thirty.

Chapter 11

'Off then.' Ernest struggled to get his arm into the jacket sleeve and attempting a half wave of departure.

A rush of cold air swept in as the door was opened; Rita gave a shiver and wrapped her cardigan around her chest. It wasn't the outside temperature that sat at the season's norm; but the bone chilling dampness of the air after rain.

Roger had his head cupped between his hands; elbows resting on the newspaper, and if Ernest had been more observant he might have glimpsed the air of dejection. However all the normalities of retirement life, like lots of time; everyday needs that had no time-table vanished. Ernest was focussed, alert and suddenly felt years younger.

He glanced at his watch as he stepped out briskly down the crazy-paving path, which Rita had supervised the year before. He got into the car and turned his head slightly to look over at the back of Lisa's house, then backed the car out and spun it around in the direction past the Horseshoe. There he turned, not to the left that led through the village but the right that by-passed the main heavily travelled main road, and took the road that meandered like a long snake, enclosing part of the town's boundary.

It was by no means the quickest way to reach the police headquarters, but then Ernest had a good half-hour before his appointment.

Eventually he slowed the car down and came to a three-way stop. The junction road sign appeared more or less as it had done thirty years ago, apart from its fresh coat of paint that now covered the once rusty patches. The black lettering had been given attention, for it was bolder in size and brighter in colour. The three-fingered post giving directions to the unfamiliar. One marked Danesbury, the other Edge Road. The third he'd just come from and marked Gelsby.

It was Edge Road that held Ernest's attention, memories flicking like an old movie through his mind. He knew the road was narrower than most, though it looked as if there had been an attempt to tarmac it, however the earth's natural state was beginning to win the battle; roots that were creeping out from the hedgerow; now were erupting through the thin layer of tar and gravel.

A white van suddenly swept down the Danesbury road and turned its wheels in the direction of Gelsby. The driver saw Ernest's car. He braked; swerved a little, hand on horn, as he raised a finger.

Ernest's automatic reaction was to challenge the driver, his hand half-lifted. He had no mercy with drivers that could cause an accident, he'd seen too many, but the van speeded up again and disappeared; leaving Ernest back in the present. He checked his watch again, and drove towards the town, pondering on the fact whether or not he should have taken the number of the licence plate.

The sun had been trying desperately to find a way to show itself all morning, and eventually the grey clouds parted and let it have its short time of glory. The puddles of the police parking ground reflected the colours around and rippled as Ernest stood on the firm ground, looking ahead at the brick building. He raised his eyes to the second floor; a faint smile hovered over his lips at the sight of a broken venetian blind.

Suddenly a surge of excitement hit him, his senses alert and his steps wide and powerful. Someone opened the main door to leave, saw Ernest, stepped aside and said, 'morning gov.'

Ernest hadn't a clue who it was. Inside nothing seemed to have changed apart from a new coffee machine and the two computers that were placed on two small tables at the end of a long desk.

He did recognise the back of Jack Buzzard's head, peering into a newspaper, the computer screen blank and a pile of computer books unopened supporting a coffee cup.

Ernest coughed; finding no response, he coughed again. There was a short sigh and Sergeant Buzzard turned. His face lit up like a Christmas tree, almost tripping over the chair leg to get to the desk, immediately lifting a hinged panel.

'Good to see you gov.' His pleasure was genuine. He patted his own stomach which was slightly bulging and looked at Ernest's solid muscles. 'Guess I need more exercise,' referring to himself. 'It's all these new fangled machines these days,' glancing at the computers.

Ernest smiled; his old associate was missing the interaction of his comrades when messages were passed around by walking the length of the building and stopping here and there for a chat.

Sergeant Buzzard looked at the large round clock facing the door, and reached for the intercom. He waited for a few seconds while glancing at Ernest and then added. 'He's here, sir.' He replaced the intercom and beckoned to Ernest. 'You'll find a bit of a change in the old department gov.'

Ernest followed him through a hallway and up the stairs; the same grey tiles and cream walls didn't appear any different. However when the far door was opened it came as a bit of a shock.

Walls had been taken out and now made into one big room. Ernest noticed the windows, small with the same blinds, his old office being the third window along.

Small screen partitions separated new desks, each supporting a computer. It was a hive of activity, phones being lifted, voices shouting to be heard, machines shredding paper, fax machines running and big copying machines with a queue of people awaiting their turn.

The familiar feeling of being back in his old workplace disappeared, and Ernest's first thought was tinged with panic. He felt suddenly out of his depth and out of the world he'd known.

Sergeant Buzzard patted him on the back, guessing his reaction. 'That's why we take retirement; guess the world changes too fast at our age.'

Ernest didn't answer, but followed him down a narrow aisle of screens. They were making for a partially glazed door; a temporary sign hung a little lob sided which read Detective Chief Inspector Granger.

The upper backs of three men showed clearly through the door's window as they got closer. They all swung around in unison as Sergeant Buzzard turned the handle.

The only one sitting at the time they entered remained seated. He had the unmistakable look of an owl; big round eyes above a small beaked nose. There was no guessing as to his height; as the round body swivelled the chair a fraction to get a better look at the intruders. His gaze drifted over Sergeant Buzzard, as would fluttering wings of an insect, before it landed on Ernest. It took a moment.

'So you're the late Detective Inspector Heath.' Ernest was not comfortable with the description and returned his gaze with a raised eyebrow.

'I wouldn't say late sir; I am quite alive and kicking.'

The detective chief inspector eyed him; coming to terms with the hint of sarcasm or was it just plain speech. He paused, before deciding to go for the latter.

'Quite so.' Then waved them all to find seats, which were not forthcoming; there being only two other chairs in the room. The chief glanced up and indicated to Ernest and Sergeant Buzzard to sit down, waving the others away; his business with them done.

'This is a serious business Heath.' He leaned forward, running his tongue over his lips and swallowing. Ernest waited.

Suddenly the chief stood up, he was taller than Ernest had imagined and it came as a surprise. He momentarily wondered if he should stand also, before reminding himself he was retired. He crossed his legs.

'Sergeant Buzzard here brought it to my attention that something akin to what we are now facing happened years ago.' He stopped and waited.

Ernest nodded, but stopped short of saying anything. Let the powers that be loosen their tongues first.

Soon all the details of the recent homicide were passed on to the retired detective inspector, who secretly marvelled at the new advances that were being used to help the investigating teams.

'Now then let's hear your account.' The chief paused before adding, 'I've already heard Buzzard's account. The town will be remembering also and we will all be put in the pressure cooker.'

Ernest related every detail. Each time he tapped into the past; the events took on surprisingly clarity.

Two hours later, and one tray of tea with tea-stained cups and saucers, the chief himself not being a coffee lover; all agreements had been settled.

Ernest was to head up the investigation of the cold case homicide that happened in 1966. He was to have full access to any files relating to that investigation and after a few anxious moments was given the services of Police Sergeant Buzzard and Detective Constable Jiten Smith.

However it was only after much hand clinching and facial contortions of indecisiveness; that he was finally given the whole works. The suspended Detective Sergeant Pharies would be allowed to work alongside him. If Ernest had any idea of dance steps; he would have used them on the way back to the canteen.

After having coffee with Jack in the canteen, and agreeing on a time of their first meeting in the room to be provided, Ernest patted his old friend on the back.

'We'll do it Jack,' he said; and Jack had no doubt they would; as Heath was back in charge.

Chapter 12

It was Tuesday when he left the police headquarters. He walked with a straight back and purpose in his stride.

Sliding into the car seat he turned the key and backed out. Someone honked their horn, his foot hit the brake. A traffic officer scowled at him before getting into his vehicle.

Ernest waited, his fingers tapping the steering wheel in time to the Beatles Yellow Submarine as he began to consider the possibility of his own computer. After all one cannot move forward when working; unless one has access to up-to-date technology and information.

He liked the sound of the word working; it denoted he was still able to use the skills which he had nurtured over the years.

Keep the grey cells working his doctor had once told him, and he was the first to admit his old doctor was totally with it at eighty. Ernest washed over the fact his doctor had retired to Spain years before.

He took his hand off the wheel and patted his left pocket. Notebook safe with details he needed to start his investigation, and his new pass with Investigating Officer, under his photograph.

The detective chief inspector had promised a room would be allotted to his team; files brought out of the archives and communication devices brought in and setup. Jack had coughed at the mention of computers; a sound Ernest recognised as a discomfort. In the thrust to get his team together, he himself had the same thoughts, until he recalled that Detective Constable Smith would be fully competent in the use of computers and fax machines. Lisa too was keeping herself abreast, and had improved her computer skills a lot during her self-imposed isolation.

Ernest smiled, the thought of explaining to Lisa that she would be back on the job, so to speak, was like having a wrapped gift ready for the offering, knowing it was just what she needed.

All in all he was satisfied with the arrangements; totally committed and determined. This time a trial and verdict wasn't going to get away from him.

Rita would understand his commitment and maybe accept the days he would be out. She always understood. As for his new found relative; well life couldn't just stop for him. As he mused, the last thought didn't sit too well, as he was aware of a guilt feeling popping up that he couldn't ignore. Ernest considered taking Roger to see the family graves the next day, as his team would not be able to use the promised facilities until Thursday.

He had hit the ring road before realizing the traffic had built up and he missed his exit from the roundabout. He went around again, this time flashing his indicator early.

Ernest had long wondered why the whole world didn't just drive on the same side. It wouldn't really matter if it was left or right. He remembered listening to his history teacher on one of the few times he did; explaining that the English needed their right hand to hold their sword in battle. So if mounted on a horse, they always rode on the left side of their oncoming opponents. He mused a little on the disadvantage it would have presented for the French, and then let it go.

There was a sense of timelessness every time he entered Gelsby; the same scene hadn't changed much for centuries. Modernisation of the cottages that flanked the green had been made, and even these changes had maintained the look of all the traditional features.

He turned and drove to the left of the green, which was filled with daffodils; just about to burst from their buds. He thought of continuing to sweep around by the Horseshoe Inn and down the lane at the back of his house to park his car.

He slowed down; the thought of having to go home first before calling on Lisa didn't sit too well. Get everything rolling first was his inclination; then explain to Rita.

He drove to the top of the green which ended in front of the church's wide steps and red pillar box, turned and drove slowly down to number seven.

His car door open and with one foot about to touch the pavement; a voice boomed out. 'Heath old man; just the person I wanted to see.'

Where the hell had Frank Butterworth sprang from was mystifying and Ernest gave an inward groan.

'Can't stop Frank.' He lied; feeling not one ounce of shame. 'Appointment you know.' He didn't go as far as voicing the dentist he had in mind, as he raised his hand, indicating his teeth.

'Of course old boy, understand totally;' came back a voice of one having been there. 'I just thought you might be up for being a member on the parish council. There's a seat coming up, and with your background, just the sort of person we need. Think about it old boy.'

Ernest was so surprised; he nodded and left Frank Butterworth strolling away; his job having been efficiently accomplished.

Closing the car door with a bang, he noticed the front room curtains of number seven move, although the front door was only opened after he pushed the bell button.

'That Frank Butterworth?' Lisa questioned; popping her head around the door and looking at the retreating figure.

Ernest chuckled. 'It seems I am a pillar of society and have had the honour of being asked to be on the Gelsby Parish Council yet again.'

Lisa's eyes widened, giving him a quizzical look.

'And?' asked Lisa. Ernest couldn't resist just shrugging; leaving a total look of disbelief and amazement on her face. 'So is this visit to cheer me up, or has Rita sent you to check on me?' She let him follow her down the hallway.

'Neither lass;' his statement made her turn and look at him sharply, the pale complexion seemed paler, her hair bedraggled. She gave a nervous cough and frowned.

'What then?' she asked, as if there wasn't anything else he could come up with.

'Feel like being part of an investigation team; doing some detective work like you've been trained for.'

Lisa stared at her old boss. Was he hinting she was back in harness again, however she quickly realized they wouldn't have sent a retired cop to tell her that her suspension was over, before asking. 'What the hell are you blabbing about Ernest?'

'Got a bottle of wine Lisa?' he asked nonchanently. She nodded, her eyes squinting with questions.

'Pour a couple of glasses lass and I'll tell you.'

She stared at him for a moment, took a laboured in-breath and indicated to the living room. Ernest had already made himself comfortable in the armchair her mother had sat in for so many years. He took the glass she offered and held it up clicking the side of her glass before saying. 'We have a case Lisa.'

Her glass wobbled slightly, her mouth opening as if about to speak. Ernest held up his hand and told her to sit.

'I've been asked to head up a cold case, and you are going to be part of that team.' He waited for a reaction, but she only stared at him; disbelief at what she was hearing.

'What cold case? And what the hell do I know about things that happened way back. I'm not a bloody historian for heavens sake.' Blotches were beginning to appear on her cheeks.

Ernest sipped his wine, sat back and grinned. 'But the case has a lot to do with the very recent one; it's a copy-cat.'

Lisa's face changed, she looked interested and plonked herself down opposite him. 'Go on gov.'

He now had her full undivided attention; starting with his talk to the detective chief inspector and to the team that had been assigned to him.

Ernest mentioned 'Old Jack', and Lisa guessed he was referring to Sergeant Buzzard.'

He nodded, before adding; 'and yourself.' He paused, before deciding to be truthful. 'Took some time to persuade the powers that be, but I insisted you knew the way I worked and you are a good cop.' Ernest failed to add however that he wasn't interested in any agreement if he couldn't pick his own team.

'Really,' she sat up and looked impressed; colour beginning to come back to her cheeks and her eyes brightened; the energy that had been sapped in her despondency was now flowing back and giving life.

He nodded, took another sip and beamed back

'We also have Detective Constable Jiten Smith with us.' Lisa's only response was a short gasp.

'So my dear, on Thursday morning I want you ready and waiting at 8.30 am, and we will start opening the files on the murder that happened long ago and was never solved.'

He stood up and grinned, placing his glass down on the nearby table, he touched his forehead in a farewell salute. 'Now I have to inform my beloved wife that I am back at work.' His actions were a bit too cocky and Lisa; sensitive always to the people she respected most in the world, just smiled; knowing Rita would be only too pleased to see her man doing the thing he liked best.

Lisa however wasn't so sure about his brother's reaction.

Chapter 13

Rita took Ernest's news as if it was nothing out of the normal. He noted her pride and total acceptance of his abilities to produce a result. It never failed to amaze him, and gave him the feeling he could accomplish anything with Rita by his side.

He watched her slightly plump figure as she ironed his shirt; the once dark hair now showing signs of grey and a few lines around the eyes. She'd aged well, and to him she was the most beautiful woman in the world. It still blew his mind that she had helped the small rebel as a child; whose shoes always had holes in, and his hand-me-down clothing too small for comfort.

He'd rebelled at his home life and at the looks that told him he wasn't the sort of child parents wanted their children to play with; often seeking attention by fighting and finding ways to disturb class-room routines. All had been against him; the strapping at home and canning at school had only promoted his aggression.

He glanced at Rita again, he'd never puzzled out why she had championed him; and made him feel like some heraldic knight in her presence. It always amazed him yet underneath he well new the answer. Rita always championed the underdog while seeing the potential in all. She had the gift of empathy.

Both had been victims; him from his survival instincts and her from finding her earlier life so full of emotional fears. Sometimes he thought there must be a God, for he had brought them together again.

The thought of God turned his thoughts back to Frank Butterworth and he gave a little chuckle out-loud. Rita looked up, hot iron raised and steaming; a quizzical look on her face. He smiled and threw his head back looking at the ceiling for a few seconds before satisfying her curiosity. 'Frank Butterworth suggests I go on the parish council.' There he'd said it, and waited for the laugh that didn't come.

She was looking at him seriously, 'and?' It was not the response he'd expected.

'Me?' he gave a half-laugh this time, not quite understanding the affirmative suggestion behind her statement.

'And why not luv.' She lowered the iron, looked at him for a moment, before continuing to press a shirt. 'Why?'

Ernest banged has hands on the table and stood up. 'Because I don't believe in all that religious stuff, do I, and whatever I am; I'm no hypocrite.'

Rita didn't even blink, her voice was soft. 'But you came to church with me.' He shrugged and changed the subject

'Where's big bro?' even he surprised himself at his apparent warming acceptance of their new-found relative.

'Gone for a stroll,' she offered; followed by a hint of a suggestion; 'likes to keep in shape.' It was lost on her husband who was now staring at the clock.

'I think I'll take him to St. John's Church to look around.' He waited for her surprise at his suggestion. Getting none he took charge of the idea. 'Let him get a look at the family graves,' he carried on.

Rita nodded and hung a shirt on a hanger. Ernest noted it was Roger's, not his.

The weather was mild, and the sky a non descriptive grey as Ernest and his brother settled in the car. A few curtains moved, and the hedge clippers of the keen gardening neighbour next door remained hanging open in his hand as he watched the car pass; the gossip around the village having not quite caught up with the identity of the newcomer staying at number eleven.

'Ok?' questioned Ernest as Roger moved his seat further back. They skirted the town centre by taking the ring road, and then entered a long road edged with terraced houses that lined up like an uninterrupted wall with windows uniformly placed; one down plus door, and two up to each residence. Ernest slowed down at number 31. 'Gran's house.' He stated, with a slight edge of sentiment in his tone. 'She was alright was our gran.'

Roger leaned sideways to get a better view. 'Our mother's mother?' he questioned. Ernest nodded and drove on, not wanting to talk about his gran; he still missed her.

Suddenly he turned to the left, and the tyres bumped off the tarmac paved road. Four more terraced houses stood vacant and neglected, the house opposite to them had been pulled down.

Ernest stopped, he didn't say anything. Both looked to the right with their own thoughts until Roger broke the silence.

'Which one?' he asked. Ernest pointed to the last of the cottages; memories of his own childhood there flooding back like a wave.

Neither spoke; each involved with their own private thoughts.

'Where's the church, is it nearby?' Roger broke the silence, as Ernest turned the car around.

Two minutes along the road and St. John's appeared, its stone wall edging the pavement and the once iron gates still lost to the 1940's war effort; leaving just two tall stone pillars.

Ernest waited for the traffic to ease, then swinging to the right; he drove his car into a parking lot of a pottery factory outlet opposite.

Nothing was said as they got out and stood awaiting a break in the traffic to cross the road.

Eventually they did and passed through the church's gateway, finding their way along the flag stones that once were the headstones of graves; now worn with age and moss covered.

Ernest led, with his brother a few steps behind, so that when the leader stopped, it made Roger break his stride too.

'Where are they?' Roger was referring to their parent's grave, not realizing that Ernest had a major problem. He'd never been there since his father died suddenly at the age of fifty-nine. After which he'd been called up for his national service. He had no idea what year his step mother had died, nor did he want to know.

His instinct took him to the edge of the graveyard. He remembered that, plus the fact the grave was somewhere behind that of a soldier called Bennett, who had died in World War 1. Apart from that, he was at a loss, owing to the fact that there was no grave stone on their family's grave.

He led the way, looking for the name of Bennett, and for a moment or two he thought it a useless journey. Then he spotted it.

Corporal Peter Bennett
Born December 26, 1898
Died Jan 6, 1919
Aged 21 years

He gazed at the grassy plots behind it, an area generally unmarked by stones; that merged with the other somewhat neglected and overgrown grave sites around.

Ernest stopped. 'That's it,' was all he said. Not knowing whether his step mother lay there too, or whether it was just their parents.

Then hit him like a thunderbolt. These were not just his parents, but their parents. Yet Roger had, in a way, suffered more than he had. Whether it was for better or worse, Roger had never known his true parents.

It was an odd feeling that would take some getting used to. He wasn't alone anymore, and in a way they both had been victims of two people, whose genes they shared.

Ernest realized that his gran knew about the other child, and she had lived with her secret and heartache till she died. Gran; who had held him close, stroked his hair; baked special goodies for him whenever he called around. Gran would have suffered as his own mother had; always knowing she had had two grandsons, not one.

However there were no such thoughts or feelings that arose of his father; only the futile hope for acceptance and praise. However his growing years had taught him quickly that such hopes would never be forthcoming.

Ernest felt a hand on his shoulder; he turned and saw tears in Roger's eyes. He paced his own hand over it and gave a little squeeze.

Roger was the first to speak. 'Okay bro, I think we deserve a pint, don't you?'

It was the best suggestion of the day and soon the car was finding its way out of the town's boundaries to a little pub on the Leek road.

So much had happened during the last few days, but the thing that would remain in Ernest's memory was that he ordered two pints from the publican saying, 'Two, one for my brother and one for me.' Silently; each with their own memories, they drank to a new beginning and their new-found relationship.

Chapter 14

Surprisingly Ernest slept well and heavily, hardly stirring in bed. Rita begged to differ and complained of his snoring, but dismissed it and patted his arm.

'You must have been dreaming,' he said and leapt out of the bed with surprising energy for his age. Rita lay back on the pillow, arms folded behind her head and watched him dressing. He still had a fine figure, broad shoulders that spoke of strength. On odd occasions she regretted the fact that she'd never held a baby in her arms that would resemble them both, but past events were now long laid to rest. They were together and she still marvelled the fact. What had gone had gone; even the occasional twinge of jealousy towards his first wife, but then reminded herself that she had been partly to blame for that.

Ernest pulled his shirt halfway over his head, saw her looking at him and winked.

'Don't get up luv,' he told her gently. 'I'll get something to eat on the way.' Ernest bent over to let her smaller fingers fasten his top shirt button, before adding 'and don't let our Roger wear you out.'

He closed the door leaving Rita smiling at his use of the word 'our.'

At number seven, Lisa was just pulling her back door closed; turning the handle and giving it a little push to make sure the lock was engaged.

She saw Ernest's car and waved, scurrying down the overgrown path to the rickety gate that needed a lift up and a tug before it opened.

Ernest started the engine, the noise bringing the parting of curtains from the upstairs back windows of one or two of the other cottages.

'Ok?' was all he said, giving Lisa a quick look of admiration. She looked good; better than he'd seen her look for ages. The pink sweater suited her and the black jacket better than the purple one she seemed to prize.

Lisa gripped her bulging bag tightly, her knuckles slightly white. Although Ernest had often asked her what the hell she had in it, she had always somehow managed to produce whatever was needed; from maps to a small microscope and always a cough-drop or two.

'Work James and don't spare the horses,' said Lisa, wrapping on the car's dashboard, recalling her grandfather's old saying, but changing the word home to work.

Ernest glanced over to her and smiled at her enthusiasm whilst silently calculating her age, coming up with the fact she must have been about one year old in 1966.

'Did you ever hear about Jennie Knowles when you were growing up?'

Lisa shook her head. 'Not really, just knew someone had been murdered by the Maidenstone, but for me it happened in the olden days and I never thought about it.' Ernest cleared his throat loudly; making a grunt in the process.

Lisa turned. 'Sorry Ernest, didn't mean to say you were an oldie.' Then like magic she laughed; before adding, 'learning all the time.'

Ernest picked up a bag of donuts and coffee from a quiet cafe and slid once again into the snake-like stream of cars; a few entering the town, but most making for the Manchester Road and the city beyond.

The last decade or so had seen a decline in the local industry. Cotton mills had closed one by one, leaving no alternative for the town's people but to seek work further afield. The city once considered a long way to travel; now was no more than a computer hop away on the wider roads and more cars owned.

However like a two-sided coin, it had also brought city dwellers seeking homes that gave them access to land and views, clean air and a more tranquil life. So it was inevitable that a ring-road skirting Danesbury would have to be provided and the once-narrow town's main street made into a no-traffic area. The tarmac paving was dug up and replaced with flat brick paving, flower troughs and outdoor cafés with chairs and round tables provided. Carefully planned, and although busy; it was rated successful, with everyone now putting up with the lines of nose-to-tail traffic in and out of town.

Ernest turned off; winding his way along some back streets with empty houses awaiting demolition, past the town's old mortuary for a long-promised new building with much better facilities. Any building would have been an improvement; for the old structure was equally depressing for those having to visit to identify a loved one.

Like a homing pigeon, Ernest cruised into the car-park of the police headquarters. He stopped, looked at Lisa, patted her knee and took the keys out of the ignition. If it had been anyone else but Ernest, she would have started to bristle, but now found it rather comforting. He got out to open her door; and standing together they both looked up at the building.

She was dreading the walk through the familiar building, knowing that tongues would start wagging; voicing their opinions on why she was there and bets placed on whether the suspension had ended or . . . . She didn't want to think anymore.

Gritting her teeth and throwing back her shoulders, she followed Ernest through the main doors; defying anyone to see her slight limp.

Imagination is a great blessing, the best and worst can come to terms within the mind and the bodily defences or stimulations touched on. Yet sometimes it turns tail and leaves bewilderment.

Sergeant Buzzard jumped up, knocking the phone off its base. He picked it up as if it was an everyday occurrence and slammed it down before opening the hinged top of the long counter.

Lisa was suddenly aware of his age lines and thinning hair. She'd never had much faith in the quality of his observations. He's getting old, was all the image told her, leaving her wondering about this venture she'd found herself in.

Sergeant Buzzard walked passed them, after giving a welcoming nod, before opening the door leading to the corridor that Ernest had last walked on his retirement. He stopped abruptly forcing Ernest and Lisa to bang into each other as the door swung to behind them.

Producing a ring of keys, Sergeant Buzzard inserted one into the lock of the door on the right; turning it and pushing it open. He stood aside awaiting the two to enter.

Ernest's reaction was amazement for the store-room he had used many times had been transformed. The frames that had once held files and boxes had gone, the blinds over the windows removed, leaving clear glass.

On closer inspection it looked as if the room had been painted from top to bottom; a desk plus file cabinets, four chairs, a computer and a machine he wasn't quite sure about.

To the right a large white paper flip board, with a glass jar full of coloured pens, and to his disbelief, recognised the carpet under his feet, which had once belonged in the superintendant's office, no doubt an excuse for the Super to obtain a new one.

He looked at Sergeant Buzzard for an explanation. Surely all this hadn't been achieved in the last couple of days; just for him and his team. Buzzard understood his old boss's quizzical look and immediately offered an explanation.

'The store room is now where the file room was. That's now being used for videos and computer files, because the room we used had been enlarged to make more room for officer's desks.'

Ernest and Lisa stared at him, both wondering if it would have been better if he'd retired earlier, and perhaps assigned someone else.

'Nice isn't it.' Buzzard looked around as if he had orchestrated the whole thing, before adding, 'the chief didn't think it a good idea to put a Cold Case Team notice up outside on the door.' Buzzard touched the side of his nose, tapping it a couple of times. 'Best keep it quiet,' he said.

Lisa's face reddened, and nearly asked who does he think we are . . . , the bloody secret service. Ernest; anticipating her thoughts and wishing to pacify the developing situation, butted in.

'Great,' he turned around taking it all in. 'Great, just what we need. Now where's Detective Constable Jiten Smith?' Lisa coughed and cleared her throat.

'I'll call him.' To the amazement of his superiors, Jack took out a cell phone from his uniform pocket, used his thumb nail to flick it open and placed it to his ear after dialling.

'They are here,' was all he said; flicking the lid down with the dexterity of a teenager.

Ernest glanced at Lisa, who shrugged. It had been a day of surprises.

Lisa turned her attention to a pile of boxes in one corner, all marked clearly KNOWLES 1966.

Ernest nodded; the signal for her to get on with it and she bent over to tear off the cello tape holding the contents in.

The door flew open bringing a smell of disinfectant followed by a cleaning woman. She looked at them blankly and then retreated almost backing into D.C. Smith.

At last the team members were together and all they had to do was fit the pieces of the long ago unsolved puzzle together.

Ernest had no doubt this time he would succeed. Not everyone was given a second chance.

Chapter 15

The next day Sergeant Buzzard entered the police building much the same way as he had done for most of his life. He looked down at the well used door mat and wiped each foot of his size twelve's on it three times. He'd witnessed many changes in his career, more rooms added, all the small paned windows replaced, glass doors that swung with a touch. Then there had been the things that didn't change, like his old coffee mug the department had presented him with after twenty years of service. And for those that knew him well; his habits had remained unchanged.

He accepted change, that is it if didn't touch on him too personally; like his place behind the counter, where he knew every inch. Nothing frazzled him; the drunks, the swearing and the threats. He'd seen it all before and coped.

Someone behind him clapped him on the back; he turned sharply to be faced with a colleague of long standing, now in charge of Traffic Control.

'Hear you've been snatched up by the big-boy,' his laugh was broken by a cough, as a peppermint almost went down the wrong way. He spit it out and gazed at the round white sweet in his hand, before adding. 'Young Skelton here will keep things going on the desk, although he might have trouble with the ladies.' The sergeant found himself staring at a young police officer standing before him. What's more, he didn't even know him.

The ladies his colleague was referring to were the local prostitutes, who had over time had gained some rapport with the older officers, often getting advice and sympathy.

'Wizard on the computer they tell me,' his colleague continued; before striding off, still making a few throat-clearing sounds.

Sergeant Buzzard glanced over at the computer, already lit up and humming. He raised his hand to the young officer now in charge and made for the side door, feeling a little depressed. Three heads looked up as door of the cold-case room opened and Sergeant Buzzard entered. Ernest was drawing lines down the flip-board; Jiten's fingers flying across the new computer keys and Lisa was opening boxes of files.

Five minutes later; Ernest gathered his team around him. 'Here we have the players and the stage,' said Ernest, pointing to the flipchart. 'The players being those being interviewed; and the stage being the place searched for evidence.'

He then pointed to another column which remained blank. 'Here,' he looked at the intent faces awaiting more to come. 'Here,' he repeated, tapping the board. The top came off his marker pen; rolled on the floor and was ignored. 'I want the names of those not interviewed, but who are in some ways mentioned in the files. Anyone, no matter how little they might know. Every piece is linked in the overall show.'

Lisa half smiled, her gov. had become quite expressive in his descriptions. Ernest's eyes flicked towards her; she flushed and stifled a nervous cough.

'Pharies here will give you each a file of the homicide; which I believe Detective Constable Smith, has already copied.'

Jiten nodded.

Ernest put down his marker. 'Good, well now I suggest coffee and a good read.'

It must have appeared strange to the young police officer that brought in the morning paper, to find four people sipping coffee and reading, two with their feet up on a pile of boxes and the others; their heads supported by their hands and elbows on a desk that was piled high with folders. There was a distinct smell of aged paper and damp mingling with the rising heat from the radiators.

By noon Sergeant Buzzard's back was beginning to ache, and nobody objected to him offering to fetch sandwiches and coffee from the canteen. Orders quickly written down in his notebook, he left, leaving Jiten to raise one eyebrow and give a wisp of a smile as he looked in Lisa's direction. She grinned, they both knew not to expect immediate service, as Buzzard would be around some table challenging his cronies and enlightening them to the importance of his new position.

Later the sun stole the lime-light by shining directly on the place where Ernest stood. He shaded his eyes; Lisa lowered the blind before they were ready to begin.

Slowly Ernest wrote the name of the victim.

Jennie Knowles, then her family comprising mother, Elizabeth, father Michael and lastly, Uncle Alan Knowles, which he underlined and added D.C.I. in brackets.

There was a gasp followed by an intake of breath. Ernest looked at his team, before adding, 'It isn't unusual for families to stay in the town where they were born.' As most of his team were also born and bred in Danesbury.

'Sir,' DC Smith lifted his hand. 'Surely the DCI couldn't be part of the investigation as he would have been personally involved.'

Ernest's mouth set. 'True, but when the case was taking too long and expenses growing, he had the power to divert the investigation to other pressing needs at the time and that murder never came to any indictment.'

Lisa had been standing, back to the wall and arms folded, she suddenly found her voice.

'And you gov, did you suspect anyone?'

The retired detective inspector looked at her for a long time and then just shrugged his shoulders. 'Maybe I had a few thoughts on the subject.'

'And!' Jiten interrupted, bringing Ernest's gaze resting on him. Jiten's face would have visibly coloured, had it not been for his dark bronzed skin at the reply.

'That's not the issue here.' Ernest's gaze turned back to the flip board. 'This is a new start, new ideas, and each person's account of their investigations is vital. No preconceived ideas. I want clear minds, each person bringing a piece to the table by looking at it from their own evidence and observations of people interviewed.'

'Jack here.' He turned to the startled detective sergeant, who had just returned. 'I know you like to have a pint or two at your local. Encourage them to talk about the past. Any little detail will be welcomed that relates to the girl herself or to her family. Most of all, did they remember anyone whom they themselves regarded with suspicion; a pervert perhaps, some oddity in behaviour, gossip . . . that sort of thing.' Sergeant Buzzard nodded and patted his breast pocket only to be told . . . , 'and Jack, don't write anything down in their presence, or they will clam up like oysters.'

Ernest then turned his attention to the younger officers, 'D.C. Smith and D.S. Pharies. Take a hike up along the Edge. I suggest you carry binoculars to get distant views. Put yourself in the place of the killer. You are stalking; and where would you think to wait for your victim, perhaps a meeting could have been arranged. Use your perceptive powers; even take a stroll along Edge Road, what can you see from there? The cottages; any back windows facing in the direction of the Maidenstone?'

'Lisa, you wish say something?' Ernest stopped, seeing her mouth opening, face flushing, before she found her voice.

'What was the weather like the day she was found?' Lisa asked. All eyes were now focussed on her.

'Dry; yes very dry. It had been a hot summer and I know just what you are thinking. Were there any foot prints to show and whether the footwear was only that normally worn by hikers?'

Lisa nodded.

'The answer lass is no, and that was one of the tragedies, the ground was like silk, the sandy soil being so dry.'

She hadn't finished and he waited, a little taken aback as she fired her second question.

'Sir,' she looked straight at him. 'What are . . . , you going to do?'

Both the other men looked from one to the other; it wasn't in the books for a lower grade officer to question her superior.

However Ernest didn't appear frazzled by the question and answered promptly. 'I'm going to visit the victim's mother, Betty Knowles. The mother still lives in the same house; although she's a widow now. Quite often one remembers past events more clearly as one gets older.'

Chapter 16

Up at dawn, Ernest quietly dressed and closed the bedroom door behind him. He carefully groped his way down the dark narrow staircase, sliding his hands along the walls for balance and support in the darkness.

He stopped at the bottom step and listened. Not a sound. Tiptoeing on the wooden hall floor, he found the hall table. Bending down his hand immediately came in contact with his old brief case.

The front room door creaked little as he opened and shut it after him. Using his hands and familiarity of the room found what he was searching for and flicked on the reading light by his favourite chair.

He shivered and wished he'd put on his cardigan. The room was cold. He bent down and lit the gas fire, before settling in his chair, feet raised onto the coffee table, where two empty wine glasses and a half-eaten chocolate biscuit still remained. He slid his hand into his briefcase and with the other picked up the half biscuit; stuffing it into his mouth as he leaned sideways.

The file he brought out was marked in ink and somewhat faded. He gazed at his writing, aware of how little it had changed over the years. He retrieved his once favourite pen, still clipped to the side of the file and having a red rubber band twisted around the top, why . . . ; he hadn't a clue.

The file was dated, giving day and time in June 1966 and entitled;

Interview with family of Jennie Knowles.

Ernest didn't open it but put it down on his knees and brought out a black book, well used and some pages loose. He flicked through the pages like a homing pigeon and found what he was looking for. Names of men in the area known to be either sex offenders or anyone reported to be involved in hassling incidents of young girls; exposure, way-laying, following, or suggestive behaviour in manner or speech. Ernest ringed two. One he knew was now dead, the other seemed to have disappeared, probably driven out of town by the insinuations of others around. Ernest discounted him, he had only one leg and could never have walked along the Edge, and if the one now dead was guilty, the latest homicide was nothing to do with him.

He had already checked for any sex offenders from the past from neighbouring areas. Nothing had emerged. Ernest flicked through interviews with school teachers, friends and those that knew the girl in some way.

Lisa would be taking care of that; as Jack would with the gossip.

All at once he remembered why he kept a rubber band around his pen. Carefully he removed the band and slid it around the book's black cover to hold the loose pages together.

Picking up the rest of the file and lifting the light shade higher so he could bring more light to bear, he read his own long-ago writing; an account of the interview with the murdered girl's parents.

His memories began at opening the gate to one of the two stone cottages that were built along Edge Road. He was young then, a little arrogant and had little knowledge of grieving parents.

The Family Liaison Team had been in earlier, a far cry from the specially educated ones of today, with all their knowledge of the do's and don'ts in the grief-stricken interviews.

Ernest, having little knowledge of personal tragedy and its repercussions, was only interested in anything that could help in finding the killer.

In truth, nothing for Ernest had really changed, maybe a few rough corners had been rounded off by Rita, but when it came down to it, Ernest was still like a hound sniffing out the fox; little would shake him off the scent trail.

He glanced at the clock on the mantelshelf . . . 6.30 am. It was too early to do anything. The constable on the beat would probably be having his last cup of tea at the local cottage hospital, where he'd most likely he'd had his feet up for the last couple of hours; chatting with the night nurses. Even the police headquarters would be quiet; with the desk sergeant rubbing his eyes to stay awake.

Here he was again living and recalling the past. That local hospital, now a clinic; and the desk sergeant would probably be busy dealing with dope related offences, usually break-ins for cash needed; and prostitutes caught plying their overnight trade.

'And they say we are now better off.' Ernest sighed and leaned back. Two minutes later he was fast asleep and snoring.

However by 9.00 am, he had showered and eaten a good breakfast that Roger had offered to cook; which had turned out surprisingly good.

Ernest then phoned the house where Betty Knowles lived, and after a long silence, had persuaded her that she owed it to her dead daughter to be interviewed again.

There was a soft sob . . . , then acceptance. 'Anything she could do to help,' she'd added in a frail voice.

Ernest heard a mumble of another voice in the background, as if she was seeking advice, and he wondered who else was in the house.

Ten o'clock that morning had been agreed on, and Ernest was on his way, giving himself time to just drive around the area for a little while beforehand.

He had thought of picking up Lisa, and then decided he needed more time to think. This was his journey into the past and he wanted to keep it that way.

Let Lisa and Jiten scout the area themselves and maybe come up with another point of view. Jack would have little trouble mingling with his own generation, they would be more than willing to reminisce and Sergeant Buzzard in plain clothes, would prove no great threat; too many pints had been shared over past decades. Ernest was a great believer in letting his team have their own point of view and input, and found that his methods usually brought results.

For himself, it was a personal journey; flash-backs of opening the wooden gate, the iron door knocker and the white startled face of Betty Knowles looking terrified at his presence.

He turned a corner a little too fast and braked. After pulling himself together he continued, now concentrating on the winding road ahead.

At one point a startled crow, intent on picking at the carcass of a mouse, rose up; black wings flapping. It perched on the top of a stone wall, watched the car pass and flew down to finish its meal.

The stone walls on either side made the meandering road more dangerous. He passed a five-barred gate with a rusty broken hinge and left open to waste land. A flock of sparrows rose and flew low. 'Rain coming,' muttered Ernest, not knowing why he believed it, but his old gran had her ways and sayings that had proved their true worth over the years.

He drove slowly past a pair of semi-built cottages. He noticed a modern extension to one which looked totally out of keeping but more than likely added comfort, as the old out-building that used to provide the toilet was gone and in its place stood a greenhouse. 'I bet the soil's good for growing,' reminisced Ernest, thinking of the years when even septic tanks were not in use in the country.

Further along the ground sloped away, giving rise to extensive views over the Cheshire plains. As the Knowles cottage was built on the slope, the builder had taken full advantage by putting most of the windows at the rear of the building. As a result, the sloping path from the road to the front door gave visitors the impression that that the cottage was more roof than wall.

Nothing much else had changed. There was nowhere to park on the road side, although an attempt at a drive sloping downhill had been made at the side of the house, and just about wide enough to accommodate a light blue Accord.

Ernest couldn't visualize Betty Knowles driving as she was a timid thing and now into her late fifties. Parking the best way he could on the road side without tipping the car over, he gingerly got out. A grey skinny cat ran across his path. It stopped on the other side of the road, tail up, and they stared at each other for a second.

What is it with me and bloody cats, he mused.

Nothing much had changed since his last visit; a lifetime ago it seemed. The broken flags to the front door held more weeds and the garden was as overgrown now as it was then. A slight waft of a net curtain; then the front door creaked open.

Ernest caught his breath; he knew it was Betty Knowles but a much older edition, the once brown hair now completely white. Her gold glasses with thick lenses distorted the same brown eyes making them even larger.

The skin was wrinkled in every direction giving her a withered appearance, the mouth thin and looking a shade of purple. Her height had remained the same it seems, although the thin shoulders were now more rounded.

Ernest was afraid that gathering emotions; sadness, helplessness, would stir and bring back past memories, but he needn't have worried; for she opened the door wide and stepped aside.

'I remember you, Heath wasn't it?'

He nodded.

'Haven't changed much,' she added; as she plodded down the narrow hallway, then opened a door on the left.

Ernest closed the front door, and nearly lopped off the cat's tail as it darted in.

The room had changed, the cloth with tassels adorning the mantelshelf had gone and so had the old iron grate with its side oven for cooking and drying sticks. A tiled surround had been put in its place. The worn out wooden-armed big chair had gone too and a paisley three-piece suite now faced the fireplace.

'Sit thar sel down,' she uttered, in an old Danesbury dialect that only his age group would remember.

'I'll just put on the pot.' She left him staring around the small room.

'Why had he thought he would enter the same room?' he wondered; his vision so clear of that day thirty years ago, when he had first broken the news that her daughter was dead.

Ernest turned his head and took in a deep breath. On his right, a table held a blown-up photograph of Jennie Knowles. It was the typical school black and white, showing a pretty blonde little girl with perfect teeth beaming out at the world.

A small bunch of wild flowers freshly picked were placed in a small crown derby bowl.

Betty entered carrying a tray and two cups. She stood for a moment, her eyes following the object of his attention.

'Jennie would have been forty next Wednesday.' Sighing, she put the cups down. 'I cannot believe she would be a young woman with maybe bairns of her own and me a grandmother.'

Ernest half expected her to show a few tears, but she didn't; instead offered him a cup of strong tea.

'Mike's gone too; died suddenly, him only fifty odd at the time.'

Ernest knew she spoke of her late husband; and quickly scoured the room for a photo, but found none. He nodded in sympathy, only to be rewarded by a big smile that took years off her age.

'Our Chris is back though; he went to Australia for a time.' She chatted on and Ernest listened patiently, letting her gain his trust.

'Didn't work out though.' She looked at him over her cup. 'So one day to my surprise, he knocked on the door.' She stopped for a moment, taking a noisy sip of her tea, before adding, 'he'd come back home.'

'Chris!' asked Ernest; his memory ticking over ten to the dozen. He did recall a small lad not much older than the girl, with blonde curly hair.

'Aye our Chris; and talking of the devil . . . . ,' she got up as footsteps came along the path, 'here he comes.'

If there could have been a replica of his former detective chief inspector; he was there standing before him.

Chapter 17

A tall slender young man held out a hand. Ernest glanced down as he shook it. No wedding ring; and living at home with his mother. He slipped the observation to the back of his mind for further thought, however his mind ticked over the years that had passed.

Chris had been no more than a lad of twelve when his sister was found; add thirty years would now make him forty two. Good looking, and getting on in years, living with his mother; Ernest guessed he was probably divorced.

The young man's grip was firm and friendly. 'I remember you,' he said smiling. 'I wasn't very big in those days, and you looked so tall. Six foot are you?'

'Six foot one,' corrected Ernest.

Chris waved to a chair for Ernest to sit in, and then placed himself on the arm of another. Betty Knowles hung back by the door, seemingly unsure what was expected of her.

'Love a cuppa mam.' Chris took control like the man of the house protecting his mother, and turning to Ernest asked; 'what can I do for you.'

'Actually it's your mother I came to see,' interlocking his hands and holding Chris's gaze.

Chris stood up and looked at the doorway through which his mother had disappeared; he lowered his voice a little. 'If it's about the girl found near here, I don't want mam to be harassed by you lot again. Heavens man, she went through a nightmare when we lost our Jennie.'

'Understood sir.' Ernest raised a hand, and Chris visibly relaxed for a moment, but it was for only a moment as his visitor was intent on his mission. 'Actually it's not about the new homicide case,' he smiled trying to take away any threat of involvement. 'I'm retired now; have been for a couple of years.' The slight wave of relief that swept over Chris's face didn't last long as his eyes narrowed as if searching for clues as to why the retired detective inspector was here at all.

'It's about Jennie that I've come.'

There was a crash as a cup slipped from the trembling tray that Betty Knowles was holding. Her face was drained of colour.

'Good Lord man, now look what you've done.' Chris jumped up and put his arm around the shaking woman before leading her to a chair, and then disappearing into the kitchen to find a tea towel to mop the spilt liquid.

Ernest felt Betty's eyes on his face; he looked at her ready to offer sympathy and apologies, but was slightly unnerved by the returning cold stare in her eyes.

Her son came over to her, patted her shoulders, before standing by the fireplace and looking down at the now unwelcome visitor.

'Tell me then, what do you want from us and what are you doing asking questions if you are out of the police force?'

Ernest let the question go, but decided honesty was the best policy. 'I'm in charge of a team that is re-opening the Jennie Knowles case. We have newer technology now and it could help us. A lot of cold cases have been solved these days and we are hoping to put Jennie's death to a final rest.'

A weak cry turned their attention to Betty, her face white as death and her fingers clutching the arm of her chair.

'Sorry Mrs Knowles, but it may be the same killer, although most likely a copy-cat case, and I'm sure you of all people would want the person or persons caught.'

She nodded, and suddenly looked old and slightly confused.

Chris took over. 'What do you want to know that you haven't got already?' there was a hint of sarcasm.

'Where were you Chris?' The question seemed to take the wind out of his sails for a moment, but Ernest wanted the man to answer, not the mother of the boy like last time.

At first he appeared a little confused as he dug back into his memory before answering, 'fishing in Johnson's stream.'

'It didn't belong to the Johnson's, it was just called that,' added Betty in a monotone voice. Her visitor looked at her for a second, but nothing more was forthcoming.

'All day?' asked Ernest.

'God man, it was thirty odd years ago, and I was only a boy; I can't remember.'

'Try,' coached Ernest.

Chris screwed up his face in thought. 'I might have called at Prof Wilson's house earlier, I sometimes borrowed his binoculars, he was quite a neat person in those days; lent me fishing lures too.' He considered the statement again, and then shook his head. 'No I don't think I went there.'

Ernest turned to Betty and enquired. 'Did you go anywhere, and did anyone call?' A sudden shudder rippled through her body then her hands began to shake. Chris leaned over and held them in his own.

'It's okay mam, just answer the man, for Jennie's sake.'

Ernest knew he'd never forget the expression on Betty Knowles' face. It was if her life force was being sucked out and he wondered if maybe he'd overstepped the mark.

'No.' The answer was quite firm.

'And your husband Mike; at work all day?'

'Yes.'

'Worked long hours I'm told.'

'Yes.'

'And Jennie, how long was she gone? and did you know where she was? After all she was only ten.' He tried not to make it like an accusation, but he needn't have worried. This time she answered with more strength and conviction.

'Children around here had always been safe and often went over the style along the Edge. I always knew where they were, and they always came home for meals.'

'So you weren't worried about her absence till later?' She shook her head, looking straight at him, and Ernest remembered his own childhood in a town where nothing unusual ever happened, and everyone knew each other.

Now he was ready to go, aware of the relief on their faces for it wasn't a subject they wanted brought up, even after letting time heal the sadness. However Ernest had one more parting shot and he wasn't sure why he used it.

Standing by the front door, he turned and asked. 'Oh by the way, did Detective Chief Inspector Knowles come by that day?' he stopped, before adding, 'I mean before Jennie's body was found.'

There was a rapid intake of breath and Betty fell against her son's chest.

Ernest took the shaking of her head for a no. Again he thanked them, leaving the two staring after him as he walked to the gate.

Slipping into his driving seat of his car, he stared at the house for a few minutes, deep in his own thoughts of the last time he was there.

He manoeuvred his car off the raised bank at the side of the road and bumped onto the tarmac. There was no place to turn around apart from backing down the lane and using an entrance to a field.

Instead he drove forward some way, stopping by a style over the wall made of wood and a sign with the word Maidenstone written on it; an arrow pointing the way. A few yards beyond there was a gap in the stone wall and a worn stony path that led across the field.

He opened his window inhaling the rush of sweet fresh air that held a slight scent of bracken. He rubbed his chin; wishing he still smoked. He would have enjoyed one at that moment.

Slowly he wound up the window, did a very careful U-turn that took all his driving skills and motored back again past the Knowles cottage to the gate he'd noticed earlier.

Again he stopped, but this time got out of the car and stood by the gate and leaned on a broken hinge.

His gaze was directed up the long lane to the cottage at the other end.

He faintly recalled its inhabitant. A small man, long hair combed back in a pony tail; an intelligent face with inquiring looking eyes, which had made Ernest feel as though it was himself that was being investigated during the previous murder enquiry.

Professor William Watson or Bill as he had asked to be called was on a sabbatical from Oxford University that summer; writing a book on the Bronze Age people.

Ernest smiled to himself, funny how he had remembered that word, never been interested in ancient history, apart from the Vikings that came from comic books as a kid, not school history lessons.

He gazed over the field recalling the rundown stone house with dozens of pieces of rock by the wall, which the prof. had told him were carved by the first people of that area. Not that Ernest could see any differences from the rocks on the walls that divided the fields.

He remembered all of that but couldn't recall something more recent that stirred in his memory. He shook his head and momentarily wondered if he was too old for the job after all. However the momentary relapse didn't last long and he was satisfied with the interview he'd had with the Knowles.

Chapter 18

Lisa felt a moment of panic as her mobile rang and she tried to locate its whereabouts. Finding it eventually in her anorak pocket, she fumbled to switch it on and locate her ear under an uncombed lock of hair. As she listened, a flood of relief swept through her. The tension that had stiffened her shoulders and threatened a headache was released when she understood at that moment she wouldn't have to come under the scrutiny of her colleagues at the police headquarters.

The first meeting of the cold case team had been reasonably removed from the main floor of activity, but that wouldn't last. There would be trips to the canteen, the toilets and change-rooms, where her old colleagues would ask questions; not only of the present but also of the past, and her suspension.

'Bless you gov.' Lisa muttered into the phone and moved to the window; drawing back the curtains. She looked up; there wasn't a cloud in the sky. It wouldn't last long and she knew that; that's why the Brits were so focussed on the sky every morning.

She listened intently as Ernest spelled out what was required of her. 'Lisa I want you to take a hike along Danesbury Edge; take sandwiches and make a day of it; haversack, walking stick, binoculars and camera, that sort of thing.'

She was already picturing the four walls; that had so confined her during her suspension from the police force, falling away as he continued, 'speak to people, if any; nose around the Maidenstone, keep your eyes out for anything missed . . . , anything; no matter how insignificant. You and DC Smith must look like a couple on a days outing.'

'Jiten?' Feeling her face flushing, 'you mean you want him to go with me.'

'That's what I said.' All the authority of her old gov. had surfaced in the retired detective inspector's voice. 'Hell, I'll get him to pick you up; it's a beautiful morning.'

The phone went dead. Lisa glanced at the clock; panic now replacing her previous emotions.

'Walking shoes, where?' She opened the hall cupboard and searched on her knees for a pair of sneakers.

Half an hour later, Jiten rolled up. Leaning over, he opened the car door, grinning as he noted at her attire; thick fair-isle jumper, jeans with knees that could do with a patch, and the oldest sneakers he'd ever seen. She threw a huge canvas haversack in the back and pulled her car seat forward; waiting for him to set off.

'What?' she demanded at the hesitation to get going. Jiten grinned as he put his foot down, turning the wheel gently to the right whilst tossing a map on her lap.

'You navigate; I tend to get lost in the country.'

'I bet you do,' thought his companion, remembering he'd been brought up in the city, and the way he'd dressed confirmed her conviction; pressed pants, polished shoes and a hand-knitted sweater so neatly done, it looked as if it had all been bought at Marks and Spencer's; his mother coming to mind.

'Nice for you to be back on the job then; eh' Jiten glanced sideways at her, but her face gave nothing away.

'Turn left,' she suddenly shouted after referring to the map. He reacted swiftly, his heart beating wildly as a dog ran across the road. The collie stopped on the other side, glared at the offending machine, and sloped off through a hawthorn hedge.

They passed the cottages Ernest had been to earlier, and carried on driving; the car climbing steadily uphill. The hawthorn hedges in full flower seemed to lose height and eventually peter out, leaving only the broken stone walling. They passed one lone cottage, now derelict; the slate roof caved in and the windows smashed; the door open and lob-sided, hanging on a broken hinge.

They didn't speak; both intent on following the winding road.

Once Lisa mentioned they were on the border that separated Cheshire from Staffordshire, although it didn't seem as if the country-side recognised the marks on the map, as it all looked the same.

Still they climbed, steadily and slowly, eventually stopping as the road ended; it becoming a walking trail. Hands on the wheel, Jiten gazed at the view. It was extensive and far away he could see hills. He pointed his finger towards them, grabbing his partner's attention.

'They must be the Welsh hills,' he stated.

'Don't be bloody daft Jiten,' laughed his companion. 'We're in sodding Cheshire and looking East; not West across the Cheshire plains.'

'Come on then, let's take a better look.' He took the map off her knee and opened his car door, getting out and stretching. Lisa joined him; wrapping her arms around her chest against the chill in the air.

'Over there are the Welsh hills,' he was referring to the map and then turning around he added, 'and over there Staffordshire.

'I know that,' Lisa murmured, although in truth she didn't. Both stood awhile appraising the extensive views.

'Come on then lets do a day's work.' Jiten climbed over a clump of broken stones, turning to help his companion; before deciding that wasn't the right thing to do by the black scowl she was giving him.

Together they found the trail that for thousands of years before earlier man had walked; sandy, stony in places and windswept, but always used to travel along the edge of the high ground.

Jiten opened the map again, the wind competing for it, as he struggled to open it wider. 'We could have also taken the trail further down I guess.'

'Thanks very much,' mumbled Lisa, but the negative tone was overrated, for in truth, she was feeling good; better in fact than she had done for a long time.

Together they stood taking in the extensive views over the Cheshire plains, which had so much diversity to its history.

'Danesbury was covered by water at one time,' Lisa offered lightened up and adding a little embellishment to her school memories of local history.

'Really,' Jiten looked at her with an interest that gave Lisa a thrust of superiority.

'Oh yes, that's why there are so many sand quarries around the area.'

'And salt,' added Jiten still surveying the land.

For a moment she was ready to make some sarcastic comeback, and then remembered the names of the towns all around that ended in . . . wich, meaning salt. Clever bugger she thought, and wondered if she really knew him at all.

'Come on then.' He started off down the trail that the Neolithic and Bronze Age peoples had once travelled carrying their coracles and axes.

Lisa was enjoying her day out so much that she almost forgot their real reason for being there. However her companion hadn't, and now and then he would take out a pair of binoculars and survey the land.

Catching sight of a group of hikers lower down, he followed them with his glasses; noting they all stayed well together and were intent on keeping to the trail.

Suddenly they stopped by a fork in the path, looking at a modern sign. Jiten trained his binoculars on the sign on which was written, Bronze Age Burial Chamber.

After Lisa had taken the binoculars off him to look for herself; both were of one mind. The Maidenstone would not be far away, and neither had seen the burial chamber, although they had always known of its existence. It was a good opportunity to view their local history and it wouldn't take long. Lisa nodded; hitched up her haversack that seemed to be getting heavier, and followed Jiten.

The standing stones that made up the burial chamber were taller than both had imagined and made of local grit stone. Both well knew the stones' history. It was a burial chamber from the Bronze Age, but neither of them had ever visited it.

There was the outer chamber where the dead bodies lay before cremation. Then the ashes were passed through a hole to an inner chamber that was covered by a huge mound of stones; the hole facing east to a rising summer-solstice sun.

Whatever Lisa had thought she would get out of it didn't materialise. Stones were stones and it was all in the past anyway. She wondered where the hell the murder investigation was going by their messing around this burial chamber. Jiten however seemed totally absorbed and scouted around the area like a school boy, before Lisa's impatience had come to an end and she wanted to get on.

'Okay Smith, that's enough,' she called, wishing she'd put on stronger shoes with all the rocks that cobbled the trail. 'Let's get on with it.'

DC Smith sighed; he'd never felt so stimulated and thought maybe he'd chosen the wrong career, however he came down to earth and studied his map again.

'Just along there.' He pointed to the trail going off to the left, adding; 'that's where the Maidenstone is.'

Chapter 19

Ernest pulled the slats of the venetian blind down. They bent into a U-shape giving him a view of the back of the police building. Recycling bins piled against the high wall which he once remembered had pieces of broken glass concreted on the top to stop anyone climbing over it.

Couldn't think why they would try, but it happened, and Ernest remembered his own adventurous nature as a lad. But glass on the top of walls; he wasn't that daft.

He turned and felt the impact of an empty room, free from the interruptions and the tapping of keys. He moved to the pile of files and stood awhile gazing at them for a second, before reminding himself this was just the way he wanted it today. Quiet, no interruptions or suggestions, not yet anyway; not before he'd got his head around everything.

He'd sent Lisa and Jiten off to scout out the area around the Maidenstone and get familiar with it and . . . , he hated to admit it; but after Rita had said a good day out in the fresh air would do Lisa the world of good, it sort of fell into place.

He had asked Jack to make a list of some of his old cronies who liked a pint or two, and had even suggested a wet whistle always loosened tongues.

The file he pulled out first was the autopsy report on Jennie Knowles. The top right hand corner was stamped with Dr. Radcliffe's name. He remembered the doctor; short, cheery disposition, thinning red hair and a thick moustache. Liked his glass of whisky and died in . . . , Ernest couldn't remember; there seemed to have been so many that came and went, usually through early retirement no doubt; glad to have a few good years living in some sunny part of the world, rather than the dreary English weather. The sun broke through and produced strips of gold across the folder, as if to challenge his imagination.

The first thing he picked out from the file was a blown-up photo of the dead girl. Ernest was surprised he hadn't forgotten the image and looked at it closely to make sure; but it was already printed on his subconscious. She looked so small and frail, the printed cotton dress splashed with her blood; the child's hands folded across her chest and the legs placed straight, white ankle socks and laced up black shoes.

It was the head that Ernest's eyes rested on last. It had been imprinted on his mind for the last thirty years. Apart from the expression of pain; the injury itself was hidden. The flow of blood had formed a puddle and bits of brain had mingled in its dark pool. The injury that resulted in death had been directed at the back of the skull.

Ernest mused at what sort of person would strike a blow that killed so violently, and to then lay the victim out as if in reverence. Then there was the small bunch of flowers placed after death in her hand. He lifted the photo up; three daisies, one dandelion and a bit of heather.

Like a light bulb going on, his mind switched to the Knowles front room, where the photo of Jennie stood, and the little vase of flowers by it; wild flowers from the hedgerow or the Edge itself.

He gazed again at the young girl, wondering what a criminal psychologist would make of it. He flicked through the folder in case there was a report; he couldn't ever remember one. But food for thought; and he made a note on a blank piece of paper.

He felt his back stiffening, so he lifted his legs onto the desk and crossed them, leaning back for comfort. The rest of the folder contained a lot of medical jargon; using words like parietal, temporal and occipital. Ernest took a deep breath; words for crosswords perhaps floating across his mind.

He closed the folder and slipped it into his brief case before picking up another file of the various statements made at the time.

DS Heath Report:

Interview with Betty Knowles—Mother of the deceased,—19 July 1966, also present during the interview, her son Christopher.

I interviewed Betty Knowles at approximately 4 pm. on 19 July 1966. When I asked her what time her daughter Jennie left the house she said around about midday, after lunch.

I then asked her if she knew where her daughter was going, and wasn't she worried that she'd been gone a long time.

She, the mother, assumed Jennie was playing at number 27. That is a cottage that belongs to a Mr and Mrs Browning who have a daughter aged eleven. Note, neither family have a telephone for communication.

When again asked if she was worried by the length of time her daughter was away, she seemed surprised and said the kids were safe in the country, and then burst into tears saying they knew their way around.

The son Christopher could offer no help as he said he was fishing all day in a nearby stream for trout.

The father Mike Knowles was at work during the interview. Note: later verified by his boss that he had been there all day; leaving work about 6.30 pm. He was a van driver.

When I asked Mrs Knowles if anyone else had been around or seen, she said no, she hadn't seen anyone earlier that afternoon.

An uneasy feeling was beginning to surface in Ernest's stomach as he flicked through and read the yellowing pages and his next interview.

Interview with William Wilson.—20 July 1966

He read it once and then re-read it to make sure he hadn't missed anything. The professor, or prof., as the locals called him, was short in height. His intellect was far above the norm; holding the position of Professor of Ancient History at Oxford University for many years, before retiring early to become a recluse in a small cottage on the Edge, doing what he loved most; delving into the Neolithic and Bronze Age periods.

Ernest had interviewed him, finding that he'd taken a group of students to the Peak District that very day and had come home with them, spending the rest of the day showing his students his artefacts. Ernest remembered as he was leaving, the small man looking up at him; a frown gathering on his rather youthful face.

Ernest noted that he had arrived home at 2.30 pm following the interview with the professor, but only after nearly colliding with a car, he'd seen earlier that day near the Knowles house. He remembered seeing someone walking from that car towards the Knowles house, but had not been able to identify him.

Ernest closed his eyes. On opening them and staring at the ceiling, he sat up quickly. Something didn't gel. There were pathways of cells suddenly lighting up, processing memories and other bits of information.

He snapped the file closed and slipped it also into his briefcase. He would take his time over the remaining files of the other people interviewed. Friends, school, anyone who had known the girl had been interviewed, including some local hiking groups.

Ernest's mind turned back to that time. A young Jack Buzzard, so full of enthusiasm to be working along side him; Jack's bright red hair severely cut short to try to flatten the curls, his face still spotty and fresh.

Turning to himself and his own ambition; climbing the ladder of success quickly. Then a detective sergeant, totally dedicated and fully in control for the first time in his life. Now his life had a purpose; his first wife Jean demanded no more than his wage packet and space to run with her own career.

Rita, well Rita had already left for Canada . . . . Even now Ernest had trouble reliving that part of him, but it did remind him suddenly that the day had passed and he hadn't eaten.

He took his coat off the back of the chair, looked around the room and closed the door behind him.

What happened next surprised him and brought him out of the past, for as he entered the canteen there was a slow clapping that accelerated into a wave. Those that knew him clapped hardest and those that didn't went along with it.

Ernest raised one hand, as someone shouted. 'Welcome back.'

The lunch hour went on, as different people he knew drifted in and wanted to natter, although after awhile Ernest got the impression that they were more interested in Lisa's return to work.

He wasn't going to let it be known she was walking on the Edge with DC Smith, so he shied away from the subject and asked questions about the recent homicide instead.

Sarah Croft, one of the police liaison officers; came across and sat down. She had been on the force almost as long as he had. Never married or had kids, but was a wonder with families that had been struck by tragedy.

'Sad case.' She wrapped her hands around the hot coffee cup. He wasn't sure whether she meant the cold case or the new homicide; then decided it was the recent one. 'Must be hard to lose a child; especially like that,' she added.

Ernest sympathized with the homicide and her job.

'They must be animals,' she said with conviction; all the anger of having to listen to the parents grief spilling out.

'Aye.' Ernest leaned back on the hard chair; he could only sympathize, not having any children of his own, to truly experience those feelings. Only he would probably kill the bastard if found.

'There are times I want out.' Sarah said simply and got up leaving her drink behind as she made for the door.

Ernest sat for a few moments staring at her disappearing figure, and then got up wearily himself. Suddenly he felt quite tired.

Chapter 20

Jack Buzzard sat motionless in his armchair at home, his hands spread flat on the arms of the seat. He looked relaxed but was in fact quite tense.

Turning his head he gazed vacantly at his police uniform jacket draped over a chair. Then his broad fingers began to drum a repetitive mantra that seemed to keep in time with the loud ticking of the grandmother clock that had never kept the right time since his father died.

He crossed his legs, and then arched his buttocks to ease his back. Jack stared into space trying to get rid of the indelible moment that loomed; when he would experience everyday like this.

Last week he'd had plans; he'd redecorate, tidy up the garden and may even go on a bus tour. The latter was only a pipe dream and in reality and he knew it, for he'd never been out of Danesbury in his life and had little interest of what was on the other side of the town's boundary. Jack was a man of routine, and his work had given him that; walking the beat in the old days, familiar roads and lanes.

Being the desk sergeant gave him the same sense of comfort. He liked to natter to all that came in, whether in handcuffs or not. He'd always put the kettle on and take any offender a cup of tea before locking the cell door. What he didn't realise that perhaps a psychologist would confirm, was that through all these interactions, they had become his family. The town's folk knew him; stopped for a natter, never looked threatened.

Now the old days had gone; he knew that, just as he'd listened to his own father's tales as a policeman of giving any wayward lad a good talking too and sending him on his way.

Jack sighed, he knew it had to change, but it wasn't always for the better. Things change; like drugs coming on the scene and no enforced military call up, the latter often being the making of the town's tearaways in later life.

The real truth for his despondency had come from the fact that Heath had instructed him to stay at home till the pubs opened; wear his off-duty clothes and talk about retirement to the old guys in the pub; loosen their tongues and make them feel unthreatened.

So now he sat, waiting for the pubs to open their doors and wondering if his coming retirement wasn't such a welcome thought after all.

He leaned forward, placing his head in his hands; before raising it again, taking a deep breath and getting up. Better fill his stomach if it meant having a few pints, knowing he had a tendency to drink the odd extra one if offered.

Later, feeling a little more cheerful he started to concentrate on the job in hand. He locked his front door; pushed it twice, tried the door knob. It was a routine he'd got into after he'd been involved with so many housebreaks; usually youths looking for money or some new-fangled piece of electronic equipment. Not that anyone thinking to burgle a policeman's house would find any more easily disposable goods. Jack's money went straight into the bank with it's safe vaults, and as for electronics, he avoided the word, apart from the TV, which had never got bigger than a fifteen inch screen. Jack wasn't known as adventurous, that's why the locals never saw him as a threat; just one of them.

Ernest Heath knew what he was doing when he sent his old comrade out to fish the muddy waters of gossip.

Jack pulled on his bicycle clips from his jacket pocket. He manoeuvred the bicycle along the cobbled gitty that divided his house from the next. It had never entered Jack's head to lock his bike to prevent it being stolen. He swung himself with surprising ease onto the leather saddle, and peddled rhythmically along the road that bent and curved downhill till he reached the junction with the High Street. Here he got off his machine, looked both ways, even though the traffic didn't go though the town anymore apart from a few commercial drop offs and bicycles.

The White Cow still stood where it had for over 400 years, its name changed many times as different periods came into being from the favourite of many The King's Arms to the Tudor Arms, Royal Stag, and eventually to The White Cow; the latter still mystifying the local historians.

The pub itself appeared to be slowly disappearing into the ground, as the buildings beside it were higher and doors taller. Jack parked his bike around the back, where once the outside toilets stood, the area now flagged over and used to store the barrels.

Again the back door to the old building was low and Jack bent his head to enter, after stepping down three stone steps.

Once the room had been smoke filled and always a large fire burning in the Tudor fireplace, that sported a roasting bracket made of iron. Not anymore, an electric fire now stood, alien in the remaining surround of the old fireplace; the copper kettles and jugs shining.

The floor retained its past. Jack walked over the large flags of worn stone.

He moved like a homing pigeon to find his seat by the leaded window. The bartender, wiping the inside of a glass with a cloth, looked up and acknowledged him with one word, 'Jack'.

Jack nodded and waited for his usual glass of Newcastle Brown. The barman uttered his second word, 'early?' as he placed the beer in front of him. Jack nodded; and raised the foaming drink to his lips and sipped.

Ten minutes later, five others had joined him at the table, sliding into their usual places along side of him, like the regulars they were; each giving a quick nod of recognition to the other as they always had. Conversation was left until they had all wetted their whistles.

Bernie Collins, whose age defied even a guess, leaned forward; slim body, full head of hair and horn-rimmed glasses that hid any wrinkles around the eyes spoke first.

'Any news about . . . , he inclined his head a little towards Jack, a gesture that was picked up immediately by others.

Jack shook his head. 'They're working on it and I've every faith the bastard will be caught.'

'Can't be one of us,' Jeff Tooley chipped in with conviction; the us referring to the town's pub locals, and not the outer-towners that often came in.

'Funny lot some of those from the city.' Ben Brooks shook his bald head, his glasses edging further down his nose as he spoke. 'Drugs and I don't know what.' He sat back his piggy eyes moving from one to the other. 'Not like the old days.'

At that they all agreed, even Jack; who'd slipped from being a police officer to just being one of them. Jack found his opening by letting them discuss the latest murder victim and then slipping in like a ferret . . . , 'I was thinking more about the Knowles girl the other day; back in 1966, remember?' The last word was a question, and they all nodded and sipped their beers in silence. Jack tried again, sitting back and rolling his eyes in his head. He wasn't about to give up.

'Betty Knowles was a mate of our Joan's, you know.' added Ben Brooks. Events thirty years past for them; didn't cause any difficulties with the conversation flow.

'She was quite a looker,' Ben sighed, 'had a lot of guys after her, me included, till she fell.' They nodded, thinking back to their youth when sex became important during their awakening adolescence and many girls fell into the family way; as birth pills were still suspect, and condoms not always carried by every promiscuous male.

Or perhaps more to the fact that there was only one chemist in town and the owners were Roman Catholic and refused to carry such merchandise.

'Mike was a lot older than her.' Bernie had always been sentimental when drinking, and wasn't always listened too; apart from Jack, who today had a different agenda than merely reminiscing and gossiping.

'Courted long did they?' prompted Jack; a question aimed to keep the conversation going.

'Nar, she was quick as I recall, but never saw them spooning or ouwt else; was surprised when she upped and wed the old bugger though.' said Ben.

Chubby Bates, the man who sat by Jack; kept pushing him further into the corner, each time his big arms reached out for his glass. He was a butcher, his shop in fact just across the road and passed from father to son over a number of generations. Although no one could ever find him in the shop at his hour, and many a transaction had been made during the war years in this same snug by his father before him.

Chubby seemed always to sit in the same seat, a family seat almost, and would glare at any offender ever found sitting there. He didn't talk much, which seemed odd for a shop keeper, but his memory was sharp and he missed little. 'Maise Knowles was probably glad though.' That was all he said, but it was enough to bring the beer glasses down on the table and eyes turned to him.

Silence, they waited; knowing any word from Chubby took time and sometimes a lot of patience. 'Alan Knowles sniffed around Betty; saw them once up Brooks Lane, and they weren't bird watching.' He lifted his glass; looking at the others to see who's turn it was to buy the next round.

Jack was astonished. It wasn't often one heard any scandal about a senior police officer; years back, especially from a mouth normally shut and not very often opened.

'Alan Knowles; sure?' queried Jack, fighting to keep the police part of his life at bay.

'Sure as eggs,' Chubby nodded. 'Maise was friends of my Alice.' Chubby's wife had been dead for years, but she always seemed to come alive when Chubby spoke.

'You mean he dropped Betty for Maise; big age difference between the lassies, eh!' Jack's instincts told him to keep the conversation going, but Chubby had already closed up, and by past experience Jack knew there was no more coming this time around.

However much to his crony's surprise and himself for that matter, he brought another round; finding later it was a bad mistake, as he tried to get on his bike.

Jack walked home with mixed feelings. He had something important to add to the cold case investigation, but he also he wanted to be sick. He decided the latter the more important and bent over his bike in the gitty.

Chapter 21

Whatever Jiten had thought the Maidenstone looked like, he was disappointed. The tall lob-sided stone stood alone. No indications of other stone formations around. Nothing like the burial cairn they had visited.

He walked closer, aware that Lisa was close behind him by her mutterings and yelps as the sharp pebbles pressed into the soft canvas of her sneakers.

Whatever they had expected to find; wasn't there. Nothing but a large standing block of grit-stone with some ancient markings still showing.

Nothing was said as they both faced it, each with their own thoughts. Lisa's tumbling back to Ernest's past and the place he would never talk about, and Jiten remembering the last time he had been here, zipped up in his coverall with a team looking for any evidence that might help.

Now everything looked normal again; the blue and white tape gone, along with the crowd of individual investigation teams, each with their own agenda. How quickly the Maidenstone had returned to just the way it always was.

The winds swept across the high land making a mockery of any human interference. Jiten gazed over the landscape and its veil of spring greenery about to come, and realised how its remoteness would appear so gentle and inviting to the coming summer travellers.

Lisa coughed. He turned and grinned, she was holding one foot over her knee moving her ankle from side to side.

He joined her and dug into his haversack for the thermos, and the plastic box with sandwiches his mother had insisted he take.

Lisa took one, and bit into the fresh bread, tasting the sweet ham and tomatoes. A slight flush crossed her face as the thought of her jam sandwiches which should be offered. She decided not to, and instead poured him out a coffee; at least it was hot and sweet. Jiten drank it, trying to forget he didn't like sweet stuff; as this coffee tasted as if someone had poured half a packet of sugar into it.

So they sat, gazing at the landscape and eating, both wondering why they were here when the place had already been gone over with a toothcomb. Lisa had learned not to question her old Gov's motives from past experience and Jiten always followed instructions to the letter; not always a good thing in his companion's estimation.

A fresh breeze blew up sending a shiver through them.

'That's it,' said Lisa standing up and making an attempt to repack her bag, wondering why the hell she hadn't brought a warmer sweater.

'Best just scout around a bit,' advised her companion getting up too and throwing his bag over his slim shoulders.

Lisa turned and as she did her foot caught the edge of a rock; lost her balance and started to fall forward; two arms grabbing her before she hit the rocky ground.

He laid her head against his chest, as she gulped in air; sharp pain momentarily coming from her twisted knee.

Slowly she lifted her face; their mouths almost touching. She noticed the tender look in his blue eyes. Another inch and her composure would have dissolved. But it wasn't Lisa that drew away. Jiten patted her back and held her at arms length looking at her reassuringly.

'Ok?' he questioned.

Blood had started to flow upwards and she felt a tell-tale blush starting to show itself. Bending down she began to rub her knee again; the pain now almost gone.

'Lead on Macbeth.' Lisa was back in the saddle as her mam would have said.

Searching around, they both knew that there would be little else to find. Every inch would had been scrutinised and samples taken of anything that looked suspicious; like fragments of rock with dried blood on them, or so they thought. What was Ernest playing at? They weren't even on the recent case.

'What's this?' Lisa bent down suddenly and checked the object, before pulling out a plastic bag from her pocket and asking Jiten for a pencil.

Then she carefully edged a stone away from a small piece of material. It was dried leather, still fastened to part of a buckle.

Gingerly Lisa lifted it up with the end of the pencil and dropped it into the bag, before holding it up to get a better view of it.

Jiten came to her side peering at it closely.

'That's been around for more years than I can remember; probably off someone's bag.'

He walked away, searching the ground around by kicking his foot against clumps of bracken. Lisa put the plastic bag back into her pocket, then walked back to the Maidenstone; standing awhile looking down the trail. Jiten joined her.

'If the victim was followed . . . ,' she broke off that train of thought and looked around, before she went back to the trail once again. 'He, or she;' she said, carefully avoiding any implication of gender, 'couldn't have come from down there.'

They both gazed back at the way they had come. They had climbed the last few yards after previously negotiating a bend in the trail further down.

'It was like that all the way here,' Lisa mused. 'Anyone following her could easily have kept out of sight till the last minute.'

Jiten nodded, and they then looked around the other approaches that were visible on all sides.

'Unless it was a chance encounter, and someone was just here, in which case I doubt it was preconceived, do you?'

Jiten shook his head; agreeing the most likely scenario was that the girl was deliberately followed there. 'Still there's always the possibility of a chance encounter, or someone knew her and became too familiar.' Then "wham". Jiten made a fist and striking at the air with it to indicate the blow delivered.

Lisa paused, looked again all around her, trying to envision the type of person that would be stalking the landscape.

'I guess there's a lot of reading to do through the files of the folks interviewed.' She coughed and cleared her throat, adding, 'I wonder how many of them are still in the land of the living?'

'Oh come on Lisa,' he saw her frown at his familiarity, but she let it pass without comment as he continued. 'If the hikers then were in their late thirties; that would only makes them in their late sixties now and people are usually quite fit even at that age. There are lots of folks of that age group still in the town.'

She let him gabble on, staring at him all the time. It was true, just because her father died young and never exercised when he was alive, didn't mean he was the norm.

She shrugged her shoulders, but not before adding: 'Good job for you detective constable; interviewing the wrinklies.'

The detective constable sighed; his mood dampened by the sarcasm in her voice and the status reminder.

The landscape around was indeed very beautiful. It had sustained many generations of different peoples over the ages. Suddenly her mood changed. Whether she had caught the hurt look on Jiten's face, or the thought she may never come back to this place as a police woman; she became very aware of the moments shared and enjoyed this day. 'There used to be wolves roaming around here you know.'

Jiten looked up and grinned. She could have kicked herself. Why hadn't she remembered Jiten had been born and bred in Cheshire and he would have taken the same history lessons at school. He let it go; it wasn't the first time somebody had thought him a foreigner in the land of his birth.

'Our Krishna, my brother, told us wolves still roam around in Canada, in fact a pack of wolves had come over the frozen Ottawa river recently, and there had been an incident in their town of a small dog being killed and eaten.' He hadn't finished enjoying the look of horror on Lisa's face. 'They hunt in packs you know. A lone skier had three following him for over two miles on the trails.'

'Bloody hell,' Lisa was beginning to dislike Canada more and more. What with Rita's stories of mosquitoes in the summer and winters . . . , 30° below zero. Now wolves roaming around; she'd take the Cheshire plains any time.

'I've often thought of following him out there,' said Jiten, having a dreamy far-away look in his eye. Lisa stared at him; her heart skipped a beat.

'That's not very nice for your mam and dad; having both their children emigrate.' She didn't like the thought of it herself either.

He laughed. 'Ah, I won't, I know that,' he said as they started to walk downhill. 'Danesbury's got all I want.' His back was towards her as he said it and she felt a sense of relief as she followed him. Lisa's hand dug into her pocket, feeling the plastic bag. Well Detective Inspector Heath, she thought, consciously leaving out the retired bit. You always said it's the odd piece of the puzzle that solves it. Don't discard anything.

She smiled, and felt the best she had for a long time; eager to show her worth; cold case or not, for underneath she knew that if the first homicide was solved, the second would come to fruition quickly.

Lisa laughed, cupped her hands together and gave a wolf call. Jiten responded with the long howls; that sent small rabbits and other rodents running for cover.

Chapter 22

Ernest slipped through the main doors of the police headquarters. Nodding to the raised head above a computer screen, he took off his raincoat and gave it a little shake, immediately feeling guilty as the drops of water hit the tiled floor. Folding the raincoat inside out, he hurried down the passage way; not seeing the frowning cleaner with her mop poised over her bucket at the other end.

The cleaner sighed, as a woman entered; shaking her wet raincoat. It was going to be one of those days she thought, wringing the mop out with frustration.

Ernest and Lisa entered their assigned room, it smelt damp and Lisa waved her hand in front of her nose. It was cold too, making her teeth chatter slightly as she shivered.

'Put the radiator on,' he suggested, hanging his jacket over an old chair and dropping his rain-soaked briefcase. Lisa fiddled with the knob, waited for the iron radiator to warm up; then leaned against it and looked at Ernest.

'Well,' she said, eyeing him over for any tit-bit of information before the others came in. He tapped the side of his nose and winked; a gesture that both infuriated and excited her at the same time. He had something up his sleeve, and she knew it.

'And you?' Ernest was looking at his feet, wondering if he could dry his damp socks over the radiator, before deciding against it. Rita was always complaining his socks smelt sweaty for some reason he could never fathom.

Lisa bit her lip, trying to bring up something that Jiten and she had to offer, but all that came to mind was the still aching knee and the extensive area they had covered. Perhaps her gov. would think she was losing her touch; and that thought burnt deeply into her pride.

Damn it, she thought, her mind flicking to the small piece of strap and buckle in the plastic bag; how he's going to laugh. Still, like Ernest, she couldn't dismiss anything, so she reluctantly dug her hand into her coat pocket and threw the plastic bag on the table with a thump.

Ernest's hand shot out picking it up and holding it to a desk lamp, as the other hand flicked the switch. Bending his head to get a better view, he then got up and took it to the window. Drawing up the blinds, he looked puzzled; as Lisa's nervous cough broke the silence.

'Well you always told me not to discard anything, even if it seems insignificant.'

Ernest frowned slightly, some odd memory passing through his brain. He looked up.

'Still believe in that luv, even if it comes to nought,' he said as he handed back the article. 'Now, what's your opinion?' He eyed her keenly.

Lisa accepted the challenge, eyed the article closely and came up with her own suggestion. 'Looks like part of an old strap with a piece of rusty buckle attached; been lying there for a long time I'd say.'

She looked up and caught his smile before giving her opinion on why it was there on the trail. 'Could be a camera strap, wrist strap, haversack strap, who knows; lots of people have been walking over that trail for years and years.'

'Correct, and we are looking into a case that happened thirty years ago, right?' added Ernest.

She nodded, but still felt puzzled, it could be nothing at all to do with the homicide, yet at the same time she felt her boss was not telling her everything. It was very annoying, and her throat was starting to tickle again. If Lisa could have looked into Ernest's mind she wouldn't have been surprised to find it fitted in with other information somewhere in the files.

The door opened, and in came DC Smith carrying a rather soggy newspaper. He smiled at Lisa, who flushed and bent her head to search for a pencil that was sharp enough to write with and wasn't chewed at the end.

'So whats' it got to say?' Ernest reached out taking the offered paper. He spread it over the desk, smoothing it down with his hands and getting printers ink over his hands.

The headlines of the local paper were still causing sensationalism by announcing the town had a killer on the loose, and no young girl was safe.

Ernest's eyes travelled down quickly searching for anything that the reporter Geoff Leigh might have raised from the past. Either he knew nothing or thought a cold case not interesting enough.

Lisa clearly saw the disappointment on her gov.'s face. Ernest had wanted mention of the cold case she realised; someone who remembered something they might have otherwise kept quiet about, especially if it concerned a neighbour, or someone they knew.

The door opened once again and Sergeant Buzzard entered. Over his shoulder they caught a glimpse of the frustrated cleaner's face, gazing down at his size 13 wellington boots; it wasn't hard to understand. Lisa guessed he must have taken the short cut over the soggy grass for part of it trailed in with him.

The team acknowledged him and went back to their work, before realizing something about the sergeant was different: and noticed the silly grin on his face.

All at once Ernest knew his old colleague had something, he felt that same flutter in his stomach that he got when finding the right word in his crossword. But the sergeant intended to make the most of this new found attention. He deliberately took his time while escaping from his wet clothes, before taking out a large neatly ironed white handkerchief to wipe his face. Ernest couldn't stand it anymore; his voice had an echo of command about it.

'OK Jack, what have you got?'

Once started the police sergeant couldn't stop, and to their frustration he described every detail from his arriving at the White Cow to his leaving, although he freely admitted he was not feeling too great when he arrived home.

The one attribute that Sergeant Buzzard had was writing everything down, and after getting home he had done just that in his black book. This he took out of his pocket and stared at his somewhat wavy writing; normally quite neat, before proceeding to tell all.

Word for word, he described what went on around the pub table. Although it was irritating to have to listen to the trivia at times, there was a genuine respect for his critical recollection of the details, which unfortunately was taking so long. However the case for writing it all down had proved its worth on many occasions.

'Both Ben and Chubby said Alan Knowles had had a fling with Betty Ward as she was before being married.'

'Yes,' exclaimed Ernest, hitting the table with his fist and bringing startled looks in his direction. 'I bloody well knew there was something!'

He sat down stared at the flip chart. The room was so quiet they all would have heard the mouse crossing the floor.

'Does this mean we are onto something gov.?' ventured Lisa.

Ernest's eyes closed slightly, bringing his dark heavy eyebrows down. It took a few moments before he answered, 'Yes luv, I think it does. At least it explains a lot to me.'

But after waiting for what seemed a very long time, no more information was offered. Ernest just brought out an old file again, ordered Jiten to make some coffee and buried himself in reading, occasionally making a note or two in his book.

Only once did he come out of his self-imposed isolation, to ask Lisa to take her find to the lab. Why she didn't know; there couldn't be any finger prints on it after it had been out in the elements for so long.

The mention of the Forensic department however, brought a more positive thought to Lisa's mind.

'Gov. did the rock that killed the girl have any skin traces of the murderer on it?'

Ernest looked pleased she'd asked, but spoke to them all in answering.

'I've checked. Seems whoever it was wore gloves.'

It was late when the lights went out and the door locked behind them. A mouse scurried across the floor towards the trash bucket where an empty packet of biscuits still held crumbs; then onto a source of drinking water from the drops of rain that still shone on the tiles below the coat hanger.

Chapter 23

It was growing dusk by the time Ernest arrived back in Gelsby, the light outside the Horseshoe glowing like a beacon for those that used the lane at the back of the cottages. Someone waved; he lifted his hand not having a clue to whom he was responding.

The rain had finally stopped yet the air still held the feeling of damp cold. He shuddered, quickening his steps once leaving the car, making as fast as he could to the back door.

It was with a sense of relief that he turned the handle, the door creaking slightly as it closed behind him.

'Rita,' he called; wiping his feet on the mat that had appeared after they were married.

The kitchen light was on, he glanced at the stove, it shone brightly but nothing was placed over the oven rings. His stomach rumbled as if in sympathy and a sense of self-pity passed through him. All the time he was driving home he'd thought of a lamb chop or egg and chips awaiting his arrival. Nothing, not even the table laid.

Dejected and put out from the lack of Rita's usual administering care, he hung his coat up, kicked off his shoes and opened the front room door.

Rita sat reading the paper, her feet crossed and lying on a small stool. She looked up and smiled,

'Hello luv, how was your day?'

Ernest plonked himself down and looked around,

'Where's Roger?' as if he expected him to be hiding somewhere in the room.

There wasn't many places one could go in the town at this time, shops had closed, apart from the new mall and he wasn't likely to be looking over the shelves there. Suddenly another thought crossed his mind. He hadn't really looked to see if Roger's car was at the back, maybe he'd . . . . It was almost as if his wife could read his mind.

'He's not packed up and gone, if that's what you are thinking.' She grinned at his expression of denial.

'Roger thought he would give us both a rest and very kindly offered to pop over to the new mall and get something for dinner which he insists on cooking himself.'

How to win the heart of a fair lady, Ernest mused, but never voiced; instead he smiled and nodded. At least he had his wife and home to himself for an hour or so.

Again he was thwarted as the back door banged closed, footsteps, and a head popped around their door. Ernest spied the white plastic bag in his brother's hand.

'Stay where you both are and your dinners will be served in a tick.'

Ernest glared at Rita meaning to pull a face denoting any food taking only a "tick" to prepare wouldn't be worth eating. She wasn't looking; intent on finishing reading the evening newspaper.

'Read it luv?' she asked lifting her head.

'Aye,' he answered trying to catch the puzzle on the back page before she folded it.

'Bet it's on the BBC News.' She glanced at the clock; ten minutes to go till 7 pm.

Suddenly Ernest felt tired and his head fell back. It seemed all but a few minutes before he was being shaken on the shoulder, to find Roger standing above him holding a tray.

'The working man first.' Roger said; placing the tray across Ernest's knees, at which only Ernest could stare. A red lobster tail and claws on crusty lettuce graced his plate; a small dish of sauce on one side and chopped new potatoes on the other.

Rita's voice shrieked with delight as she clapped her hands.

'Oh Roger, I haven't had lobster for so long.' Roger bowed and left; returning with another tray for her.

'Enjoy,' he smiled, leaving to fetch his own.

Apart from the lobster tail shells and empty claws, the plates were cleaned; savouring every morsel of food, only to be assailed again with fresh strawberries and cream.

Fully satisfied and mellow, Rita tried to get up to make coffee, only to be gently pushed down as Roger started to clear away the dishes.

After he'd gone, their eyes met, each understanding what the other was thinking. Ernest backed away first, feeling a little guilty at his past behaviour.

At 7pm, the local news was turned on, and Ernest's apprehension was proved correct for it not only focussed on the recent homicide but also the past one leaving him surprised at what had been dug up.

Suddenly the face of the chief inspector appeared, giving his account of the progress that didn't add up to much.

Then Anna Booth's parents appealed to the public to help in the police inquiries if they suspected anything. Ernest leaned forward, half expecting more reference to the cold-case but to his surprise there wasn't any.

Soon there would be; that he knew, once tongues were loosened in the pubs by inquisitive reporters.

The phone rang. Rita got up and answered it. After a minute or two she called Ernest, mouthing someone's name and pointing to the phone.

Ernest leapt up.

'Hello, Ernest Heath speaking.' There was a pause, before Ernest recognised it was Geoff Leigh; the town's reporter.

'Ah Ernest.' Ernest shuddered at the familiarity. 'I know it's late but just wanted a bit of info on the Jenny Knowles case.' There was a break and an intake of breath. 'You remember that Heath don't you. Thirty years ago, and weren't you on the case yourself; the case that you never solved. It's a bit of a coincidence isn't it old boy. Sounds like the chap's on the rampage once more; any comments?'

Ernest heard a faint chuckle before he slammed down the receiver. He stood; hand on the phone for a few seconds, than told himself it was bound to be brought up. Trouble was he wasn't ready for Geoff Leigh's enthusiasm about failed homicide investigations; especially his own.

Just about to walk away, the phone rang again. Ernest lifted it up, his shoulders tense.

'Yes,' he barked into the voice piece.

The voice on the other end sounded a little off put at the tone.

'It's Frank Butterworth here; could I have a word with Mr Heath?'

'Heath here,' there was almost a resignation in Ernest's tone, one more idiot to deal with and he could relax.

'Hello, old boy.' Ernest cringed. Frank continued enthusiastically.

'Have you given anymore thought,' he stopped, momentarily before continuing, 'about joining the Gelsby Parish Council?'

Ernest sighed, his shoulders and neck were beginning to feel tight and he just wanted to have some space by getting rid of the caller.

'Yes, I'm giving it serious consideration and will let you know soon.' Ernest heard a slight gasp of pleasure at the other end.

'Good, good' the voice said, 'I'll send you the details of our next meeting old boy, cheerio for now.'

The phone went dead; leaving Ernest holding his end and wondering what he'd let himself in for. But like anything else that swirled around the one-pointed man; Ernest let it go.

Coffee was awaiting him, his paper folded neatly; the puzzle page facing him in case he wanted to test his grey cells. Rita was smiling happily and knitting the sweater she'd started for him that didn't seem to grow much past half the first sleeve; with Roger humming as he packed away the wrapping from his shopping.

Two minutes later Ernest was asleep occasionally waking himself with a snore.

A few doors away, Lisa was finishing off a micro packet dinner that tasted like nothing but dried chicken and limp spaghetti, before frantically looking for anything resembling milk to go in her coffee. Frustrated, she opened a bottle of Chardonnay, switched on the local news, whilst she poked at the apology for a meal.

One hour later found Lisa eating a packet of chocolate biscuits, finishing off the wine and watching the news channel once again; her eyes finally closing until the morning.

Chapter 24

For the very first time in his life the smell of egg and bacon did nothing to stimulate Ernest's appetite, in fact it only increased the uneasy feeling in his stomach.

He lay awhile trying to analyse the reason for feeling slightly nauseated, and could only think it must have been the custard tart that he's picked up half price at the canteen. It did taste a little stale, nothing like the ones they got from the local bakery before the supermarket helped close them down.

So much for progress he thought turning on his side and drawing his knees up to his chest.

He heard the bedroom door open, and the next minute a hand pulled back the sheet covering his face. He half opened his eyes, the cup of tea in her hand coming into focus and causing another queasy feeling. He moaned and turned over.

'Are you feeling alright luv?' Rita's voice full of concern floated down as a cool hand was laid across his forehead, then much to his surprise, she padded out of the room.

Two seconds later she was back, and something cold was stuck into his mouth and fingers on his pulse.

He gazed up at her, while mustering all the little boy appeal he could. Being administered to by one's own nurse was quite enjoyable; or would have been if his stomach felt normal.

Squinting through the eye not pushed against the pillow, he saw her gaze at the thermometer, smile a little, which he hoped was one of relief.

'You're not dying Ernest, but your temp's up a bit, so stay in bed and I'll get you some water.'

Then he felt his head being lifted, pillows puffed, and the bed-covers drawn up over him. Funnily, he felt a little better already, and a great overwhelming love for his wife enclosed him before he dropped off to sleep.

Downstairs Rita was shaking her head and smiling.

'Eaten something, tummy off,' she offered when Roger looked up from his plate full of eggs and bacon.

He nodded, fork poised in mid air before tucking into his meal again. Then with a half-eaten mouthful asked,

'Anything I can do Rita?'

She shook her head, and reached over for the toast, shaking loose the burnt pieces on her plate.

'I don't think so,' she paused then looked at him. 'Truth to tell I wonder if all this new excitement is too much for him. The trouble is once on the trail of something, so to speak, he can't let go and,' she took another bite, chewing it as she spoke. 'It's a long time ago since that little girl was killed; there cannot be any clues around now surely.'

Roger leaned forward and poured two cups of tea, offering the milk jug which she refused by holding up her hand. 'Did you know anyone involved Rita?' he asked, leaning back and sipping the hot liquid. She shook her head.

'Not really, I knew the guy as a lad that Ernest later worked for, not by friendship or anything; just knew him like most boys around.' She stopped; searching her memory awhile, before continuing.

'Good looking, very fair, rode a bike around town; had a brother and a sister who went to the USA.' She stopped, and then laughed. 'The sister went to America, not his brother; cannot remember his name, but he was a bit . . . .' Rita raised her eyebrows and slightly turned her head; a good indication to infer that the brother was slow.

'Mike Knowles.' Rita suddenly declared. 'That's his name. He used to follow his brother Alan around when they were kids; would do anything for him.'

'Once into the past, Rita began to tell Roger more about his brother Ernest and his upbringing.

'Never liked his dad, I was a bit frightened of him and his stepmother would have been happier if Ernest hadn't existed I'd say. Poor luv; if it wasn't for his old gran.'

Roger listened to the world he could have been part of, and fortunately for him wasn't, but his grandmother he never knew sounded nice and he listened carefully to anything Rita could remember about her. Then looking at the clock, she got up.

'Heavens, I didn't realise it was that time.' She looked despairingly at the table with all its dirty dishes. 'I have a dental appointment.'

Roger got up to usher her away. 'I'll do this; it will be good to help out a little.'

Rita slipped out of the kitchen, only to pop her head around the door two minutes later, 'Ernest; keep an eye on him will you,' it was more of a command than a question. Roger laughed.

'Be gone woman, the man has a dedicated doctor in this house; he will have my sole undivided attention.'

Rita gave a quiet sigh; thinking that was the last thing her husband needed.

Roger was as good as his word; the kitchen was ship-shape and Bristol fashion in no time at all. He even took a cup of tea to Ernest, who seemed to be sleeping so soundly; so it was brought downstairs again and he drank it himself.

The house suddenly seemed very quiet and lonely; there wasn't really anything to do as it wasn't his house. He wondered where the morning paper was and turned his head searching the chairs and tables. Nothing, only Ernest's folder he'd been reading the night before lay by the side of the hearth. 'Must have forgotten it,' muttered his brother; half standing up and reaching for it, the loose papers slipped out and scattered over the floor.

'Sod it,' muttered Roger; his vocab. leaving nothing to the pleasing of a sensitive ear.

One by one he checked the numbers at the top and stacked them together leaving the brown envelope to the last. It was the writing on the envelope that made him hesitate. He was looking at the autopsy report on Jennie Knowles by a Dr. Graham Radcliffe. Curiosity getting the better of him; he opened it.

Roger's eyes scouted out passages like time of death that was given as 1.0 pm. He knew that without any reliable information that the time of death is usually established by the appearance and condition of the body. He also knew that the contents of the stomach were an indicator of her last meal.

His attention was spasmodic, stopping at places of interest. He wasn't too interested in the changes to the body with the passage of time as the doctor would have been trained, as they all were, on the body's decomposition and the onset of rigor mortis. It would have also included the technique of finger pressure on the dead body to observe the change of blanching of the skin.

The doctor had recorded the death was from a blow to the head.

Roger slipped a photograph of the girl's injury from behind the report and studied it for awhile, turning it one way and the other at the same time, trying to recall what Ernest had said. 'Someone hit her on the head with a rock.'

Roger frowned and started to search through the different photos till he picked out an enlarged photo of a rock. He flicked over the report on sexual activity, remembering Ernest had said there was no evidence of that to be found.

Swabs, vaginal, penile or oral, were all negative; so were the nasal swabs collected for drugs, if suspected.

He came back to the photo of the rock again, no other blood samples or hair samples, only those of the girl's. There were no other finger or forearm skin samples on the rock . . . , nothing.

Again Roger returned to the photo of the skull and looked at the broken bones.

He seemed at last to be satisfied by his investigation and slowly placed each piece of paper in their right order, and replaced the folder back in the position he'd found it.

Treading carefully up the stairs, he opened his brother's bedroom door an inch or two and peeped at the sleeping man, before closing it gently.

Ernest heard him treading softly down each stair, a little movement in the hall, and the front door open and close, before turning over and falling off to sleep again.

When Rita arrived home the light was on; the evening still long and she'd been out much longer than intended, taking time to visit her niece and her young family at the other end of town.

The thought of Ernest not being well made her feel guilty, but her long nursing experience had told her that a good long sleep and plenty of liquids should do the trick, and if her conscience troubled her more than necessary; she remembered there was a doctor in the house.

So it was with a tinge of guilt that Rita opened the back door, but all was quiet, a couple of large tins of broth and a pizza was on the kitchen table; together with a good quality Chardonnay.

She ran the cold tap, and then filled the kettle; it had been a long day and the men had obviously survived without her.

Chapter 25

Ernest awoke the next day feeling more like his old self and quite hungry. Rita fussed around insisting he had a bowl of porridge, which he hadn't the heart to say he didn't like. However one look at her face and the big pan on the stove told him to keep quiet or the loving ministering for his welfare would be over.

Pouring a spoonful of golden syrup on top he stirred it in, and then played with the mixture before raising some to his mouth, then swallowed it with his eyes closed.

Rita had turned from the sink and was watching him. He looked up with a half-hearted smile. She sighed, cut two pieces off a fresh white loaf and popped them into the toaster, before reaching over the table and snatching his bowl away.

'I'll get you toast,' she told him with a look of martyrdom. The toaster clicked, and within minutes Ernest was spreading butter and marmalade across the crispy bread. Rita slid into a chair opposite him, sipping her tea and looking at her husband over the rim of her glasses.

Satisfied, now was a good time to tell him. She approached the subject slowly.

'They all phoned, asking about you,' she offered.

Ernest just nodded, helping himself to another slice. Rita's reference to they hadn't needed any names, but it was nice to know each one of his team had enquired about him separately.

'I've invited them all for dinner tonight.' There she'd said it; but waited for the aftershock she knew would come.

'You've what!' he stopped eating and looked at her in surprise.

Rita stood her ground, and got up, clearing the table in a burst of activity, but not looking at the face still staring at her in shock.

'Yes Ernest, I really think it would be nice,' she stopped knowing the hard part had yet to be voiced. 'Thought it would be a nice gesture,' she was beginning to repeat herself feeling a sudden flush of uncertainty cruise through her solar plexus, and, in for a penny in for a pound; she recalled the old proverb. It would be really nice for Roger to get to know faces as well as names.

She looked at the stunned face in front of her and wondered if she had maybe overstepped the mark.

'Roger getting to know Jack and Jiten?' total disbelief registering across his face.

However his wife had had her own thoughts on the matter and wasn't going to give in; not after she'd bought a whole fresh salmon.

'Yes I do.'

The stubborn face of the school-girl Rita unhinged him a little; and he felt himself becoming resigned to the suggestion. Ernest heard Roger coming downstairs, his mind flipped from the conversation with Rita to the paper probably lying on the front door mat.

'I'll leave it up to you then luv,' he said getting up, at the same time wondering why his gran's quotations kept popping into his mind; all signed and sealed.

Later, Rita left to do some shopping, and call at the bank and library; taking Roger with her. It left Ernest wondering if

Roger had already decided on a much longer stay with them after all.

Ernest's eyes rolled up into his head, as he picked up the phone, as if to detach himself from any long period Roger had in mind with them. Lisa picked up the other end. After he'd explained he was perfectly well; he had to listen to Lisa advising him not to come into work at the police headquarters; but rest and they could talk tonight.

'I'm by myself in the cold-case room, sorting through the folders on the late detective chief inspector.' she said. 'Jiten has gone to find out a little more about the professor, and Jack . . . , well Jack thought he could dig up a little more information from the gossip in The White Cow.'

Ernest mumbled something that sounded like, 'nice work if you can get it.'

It slipped over Lisa like smooth oil, and she chatted on about the amazing sight she'd witnessed when opening her front door that morning.

After hanging the phone up, and Ernest's curiosity stimulated, he moved to unlock the front door and was greeted by a waft of perfume; delicate and full of springtime memories.

The open door; framed a canvas of yellow, as he stepped to take in the vista of the village green and the blanket of fully opened daffodils. Wordsworth's poem came to mind as it always had when confronted by the sea of spring colours dancing in the gentle breeze.

A knot of people were standing by a neighbour's gate, brought out like him to witness nature's gift. Someone raised a hand and smiled. He nodded back although he hadn't a clue who it was.

For the rest of the day, he re-read the old reports again, having found Rita's old medical dictionary to help with the fanciful names, mostly derived from Latin. He never could understand why doctor's prescriptions were written in Latin.

Why use the word aqua instead of water. He guessed it was because the doctor's liked their patients to think them clever.

Roger's knowledge of some of the terminology crossed his mind, but he rejected it; best let the detectives do their own work. Up to that moment it never entered his head there wasn't much difference in the investigative skills required by both professions. He slept soundly for the rest of the day in his arm chair, until Rita and Roger came home.

The comfort and quietness of the front room suddenly became a battleground. The large oak table with all its extensions pulled out, chairs rearranged after being carried in from the kitchen and the cutlery placed and positioned, which he'd never quiet got the handle of. Roger went for a lie down, and Ernest wasn't quite sure how he himself, had ended up outside the back door with his jacket on.

Sometimes English weather has the blessing of the gods and today was one of them. Not a wisp of a cloud in the sky, the afternoon sun shone its golden rays over the range of buds and they reciprocated by turning their heads and opening; snowdrops, daffs, tulips, all responded, and the birds making calls bringing the music that delighted bird watchers.

Ernest's step lightened too, he felt good; in fact he very good indeed, his head clear, and looking forward to the evening. Rita was right, but then she always was. All of Ernest's reservations were swept away when the dinner guests started to arrive.

First Lisa, who came in through the back door, carrying something on a tray covered with a tea towel. She'd obviously made an effort with her dress and he realised she had a pair of very well shaped legs. A fact he'd never had a chance to see as she always wore pants.

She lifted her head to acknowledge him and he found himself just standing and staring at the well made-up face. Lisa looked quite beautiful.

He opened his mouth to comment, and then closed it quickly. Rita was standing behind their guest looking at him with a frown and shaking her head.

Jack and Jiten arrived within minutes of each other, the younger of the two looking less like a policeman than a young man going clubbing with his bright red shirt and gold necklace. His companion on the other hand appeared a little flushed; his hand a bit unsteady as he handed over a wine bottle.

Ernest made a mental note to ask Jiten to take Jack home afterwards. He would drive Jack's car back and come home with Lisa tomorrow. Maybe Jack should be told to hold back on the pub gossip.

Sitting around the table Ernest felt a swell of pride, without Rita in his life all would have been so different.

The conversation was stimulating, all keeping off the subject the four were involved in, and surprisingly Ernest learnt a lot more about his brother from the hospital he'd trained at; to his favourite colour, which to his secret pleasure was the same as his own.

It wasn't till the table was cleared and folded away to make more room that the subject they had all avoided was brought up, but not by anyone of them involved in the cold-case.

It was Roger that posed the question. 'How was the girl killed?' He saw the puzzled look around the table, 'the first one I mean; Jennie Knowles.'

After the initial surprise Lisa came forward with the information.

'It was a blow to the head that killed her; someone hit her hard on the back of the head with a rock.'

All heads turned from Lisa to the Roger, who was considering his next words by stroking his mouth with his hand before he stated. 'No, that's not correct; nobody hit the girl standing close by. I'm certain the rock was thrown at her.'

The clock seemed to have stopped. Rita had a flashback of waiting for the impact of a V2 rocket in the wartime. A muscle started to twitch on Roger's cheek, he leaned forward and sighed.

'I've first got to apologise to Ernest.' All eyes turned to witness the blank look on Ernest's face. 'You see I read the file that Ernest brought home.' He held up his hand as he apologized, before continuing.

'Hear me out first, then sentence and hang me,' he looked at Rita and added, 'my case is already packed and thank you for the marvellous dinner.' He sat awhile, his hands clasped on his knees as he leaned forward.

'It was the photos that interested me and the autopsy report. You see that was my own field before I retired, and the report I was reading didn't sit well with me after I saw the photos. The impact of the fracture was wrong and I would bet my reputation on it that the rock was thrown from a distance of ten feet or so.'

All heads turned to gaze at Ernest; and the other persons in the room secretly betting that there was some sort of an explosion about to erupt. Rita wondered if she should make a pot of tea, but her legs wouldn't move. The only interruption to the silence was a hint of a whisper from Lisa's nylons as she crossed her legs.

Then at last Ernest was center stage, although his performance was not what was expected. He gazed at the file pushed beside the bookcase and sighed.

'It wouldn't be the first time old Radcliffe had got it wrong.' It was obvious to the others in the room that Ernest had slipped into the past for he had taken on a blank look.

Jack's voice, though a little slurred from the many drinks he'd had, spoke up in the name of duty; but only uttered one word.

'Aye.' It was his confirmation of other past errors.

Roger was beginning to get up, but his brother waved him down.

'Sit down you old fool, I'd have done the same; no harm done.'

Lisa agreed by pointing out if it wasn't for Roger; they might not have had all the facts. Ernest again scowled at her, while Rita hid a smirk and thought this was the right time for that tray of tea.

Chapter 26

Ernest felt good, everything was moving in a one-pointed direction. His once-scattered thoughts filing themselves in pigeon holes; in some cases even labelled. There were some though that still kept floating around, taunting him with ever-changing ideas.

The driving was easier this morning; he'd placed a bet on the fact that it was the signs of spring after the long grey dismal winter. He let his side window down a couple of inches and breathed in. He felt good.

Feeling good in truth had nothing to do with the weather. It helped of course, but for Ernest to capture the sense of enthusiasm meant his quarry was in sight and just a matter of bringing it to bay.

He wound around the lanes towards the Edge like an expert, swearing he saw the very same blackbird sitting on the wall waiting for him to squash what looked like a dead hedgehog. Someone had once told him blackbirds were extremely intelligent, but he guessed it must have been ravens, which would explain why wizards always have them sitting on their shoulders.

Ernest gave his head a slight shake to bring himself back to concentrating on where he was going. He glanced at the clock on the dashboard. 'Good timing,' he mused, recollecting the professor had suggested 10 o'clock as he slowed down nearing the gateway with the broken hinge. Again Ernest wasn't about to drive his relatively clean car up the dusty lane, so he pulled up on the side of the road, where a fair amount of grassy land gently sloped away and started the walk up to the cottage.

As he got closer, it was like taking a stroll back in time. There was no sign of husbandry, the ground right up to the door was all field. Even the wild grass hadn't been cut around the slab of stone used as a step. Leaning against the grey stone walls of the cottage were large grit stone slabs with markings of unintelligible design; the weeds and grass again framing the lower ends. Ernest stood awhile, trying to decide whether they were old gravestones.

A voice broke his meditation, his head jerked up. Leaning by the open door was a small wizened man; his grey hair seemed to grow in clumps giving an oddity to the shape of his head. He was clean shaven, which surprised Ernest; although he didn't know why.

William Wilson had always been small; but seemed to have shrunk further over the years. He wore jeans with the bottoms turned up, bringing back memories of the 1950's. His flannel shirt was plaid; the tartan design bright, but the collar worn; the bottom and top buttons missing.

They stood staring at each other for a second, each with their own thoughts of their meeting years earlier. With a nod of the prof's head, Ernest followed him through the door.

Nothing had changed; the same but older looking large kitchen range with its central pipe, the long wooden table and chairs, the bookcase filled to over-flowing by piles of reading material stacked up beside it. The shelves with broken pottery and rusty metal objects and a few bones that Ernest couldn't tell whether they were of the human kind or animal.

He glanced back at the table once again, papers scattered willy-nilly around with open ancient maps and half-eaten biscuits.

Ernest guessed this was the tidiest the room had been for a long time, as he noted a big iron scuttle filled with fast food packets, squeezed up paper and what looked like cat feces. Yes, he was right; a large black cat was crouching under the chair with the posture and expression of satisfaction.

The bright-eyed man pulled out a chair and indicated with the nod of his head to the one opposite him at the table for his guest to sit.

'I remember you,' he said looking at Ernest with interest. 'A fine fellow you were.' Did Ernest note a little sigh, he wasn't sure, but did remember a long time ago wondering if Bill Wilson was gay. Gay wasn't used or even talked about in those days, and the moment of unease passed.

'So what can I do you for?' Bill sat directly opposite to him, his hands spread out on the table, trembling a little as he leaned forward.

'I'm looking into the Jennie Knowles case again.' There was no point in beating about the bush, thought Ernest; 'I wondered if you could recall anything that might help with the investigation.'

Two bright eyes stared at him, before Bill pushed back his chair; almost knocking it over in his haste.

'First I'd like a coffee, how about you?'

Ernest nodded, and leaned back as much as he could in the hard seat, watching his host actually pump water. His eyes roamed around the white dirty walls, an old print in a black frame tilted slightly, looking as if it might fall at any minute, as did a home made rack with bits and pieces hanging on the pegs.

A battered haversack; pockets torn, a hikers pole with a leather strap, a couple of broken pegs and a binocular case; its strap broken and tied together with string. Bill came back with two large mugs and followed his visitor's gaze.

'Should get rid of some of my junk,' he said wistfully, 'but they're all part of my life.'

Ernest's heart was beginning to beat quickly; his hand shaking a little as he lifted the hot mug. The blue eyes watched; a smile on the face of the owner as if he had caught a fly in his web and not the other way around, as he answered the question he knew would come.

'Yes, I'm a keen birdwatcher as well as my interest in the Bronze Age, and your next question will be whether I often go on the Edge? And do I spy, or have I ever spied on courting couples?' The answer is yes, I have been known to occasionally in my youth; but it was more of an interest in the male species than the female.' He smiled and warmed his hands around the mug. 'Now does that answer your questions?'

Ernest blushed and looked little shamefaced.

'They say Bill Wilson is smart professor.' Ernest gave the man opposite his full title, to emphasize his meaning.

'Yes, it has been said,' the professor admitted without pride.

'Who else likes to bird watch around here?' Ernest asked; hoping to find out other possible members of some club maybe.

The prof. shrugged his shoulders.

'They would come and go, mostly in groups for a day out.' He thought for a while. 'Young Chris, he was interested, used to come here a lot as a kid.' The prof's voice softened. 'He would often borrow my binoculars; very keen he was.' Silence then, 'lovely boy he was; missed him when he upped and went to Aussie land.'

Ernest kept his eyes down, again a slight rush of adrenaline threatened to make him too eager for any other forthcoming bits of information. 'Did he ever mention his sister to you?'

Once again the prof. out-smarted him. 'Fishing for suspects are you?' So the cards are out on the table, thought Ernest, and he sat straight up and decided to come clean.

'That's right, it's been thirty years since that young lass was killed. I think it's time Jennie Knowles got her revenge, don't you?'

They stared at each other for a few minutes before Bill turned away and pushed out his hand to collect the two mugs. Ernest watched him as he refilled them before sitting down and sliding one across the table to him.

'So this is all about young Jennie.' Ernest felt his host looked a little relieved as the prof continued. 'I'll tell you all I know. Jennie's father; Mike Knowles wasn't the brightest of the bunch, but I suspect wasn't daft either. I'd seen him a few times creeping around whenever his brother came visiting his wife.'

He gazed at Ernest, waiting for him to register the fact that Mike Knowles' brother was more friendly with his sister-in-law than he should have been. Ernest nodded and took out his notebook; pencil poised. The man before him started to talk.

Ernest's face remained non-committal, but recalled having his own fleeting memories of the detective inspector comforting the girl's mother.

'The boy Chris enjoyed his uncle coming around; I think he made quite a fuss of him.' The prof. stopped before adding, 'Funny how the two brothers didn't look much alike, the uncle was quite a looker.' The prof. held up his two hands in surrender, adding 'Just my opinion of course.'

The room remained silent for awhile before Bill Wilson got up, lifted the lid of the stove before filling it with coke. He shivered; the days were getting chilly. He looked at his watch. 'If that's it, I need to get back to the book that I am writing.'

Ernest took the hint and closed his notebook; knowing that was all he was going to get out of him.

Chapter 27

The long reception counter at the police headquarters was busy when Ernest walked in.

A traffic cop was trying to keep the peace between two angry individuals, while a local drunk was singing 'Sonny Boy' in an Irish dialect that became broader as the singing went on.

Someone called Ernest's name, a voice slightly familiar; but from a long time back. He turned. Over the heads of the others he caught a glimpse of a familiar but much older face. He raised his hand but it wasn't until he closed the door behind him that he remembered; Elizabeth Newton or Bizzie Lizzie as she was known by at the time.

'Couldn't be,' Ernest muttered, turning again to open the door a little way and peering over to the other side of the room. 'Yes it was,' he couldn't believe she was still on the game. It seemed years ago since he used to bring her in, but there was little doubt in his mind; the red hair, posture, the face now much thinner.

'She'd be now . . . ,' Ernest counted the years, as he closed the cold case room door again; standing a moment. 'Hell,' mused Ernest, 'she must have been so much younger in those days than any of them had realized.'

There was a murmur of greeting as he turned; closing the door behind him. Jack had his big feet upon the desk, drinking coffee. Lisa and Jiten had their heads close together; studying a map.

'Don't get up,' Ernest said, a little sarcastically and no-one did. He sighed and pushed Jack's feet off his desk.

'OK, OK, let's get on with it,' he strolled over to the flip board. 'Let's start again.' Three pair of eyes watched as he wrote.

Detective Chief Inspector Knowles; then crossed out the word Chief.

Ernest turned to his team, 'Alan Knowles was only a thirty one year old detective inspector in 1966. What do we know of him?'

Lisa spoke up. 'He married the super's daughter.' Two faces looked quizzically at her; both wondering where she was going with that statement. However Ernest knew full well what her intentions were.

'Correct Lisa,' he nodded pleased with his protégé, then probed a little more.

'So let's look at what kind of man Detective Inspector Alan Knowles was at the time he took command of the Jennie Knowles' homicide.'

Again Lisa's voice was loud and clear. 'Ambitious.'

'Why do you think that, what evidence do you have?' asked Ernest.

'Because he was going nowhere in his career before his marriage; sir.' Lisa tapped the file in front of her; there wasn't so much as even an embarrassing blush at having got her hands on his personal file.

Ernest glanced at Jack, who to his relief also showed not the slightest sign of embarrassment at his lack of career progress. Jack had always been quite happy just where he was, and had actually turned down a lift up the ladder, for it would have involved a transfer to another division.

Ernest quickly got back to the thrust of his line of questioning. 'What else do we know of him outside his line of work?' He was looking straight at Jack, who took up the challenge straight away; understanding where it was all leading to.

'As I said before sir,' Jack still couldn't get out of the habit of addressing Ernest as he had when they worked together. 'Alan Knowles had a reputation for liking young ladies.'

Ernest interrupted, 'Betty was only just turned seventeen; unmarried and quite a good looker when Alan Knowles first sought her out. From what I've also heard, he was even known to pursue younger ones.'

'Dirty old man,' said Lisa, clearly angry.

Ernest turned to her adding, 'Yes, quite so; but just keep in mind Jennie Knowles, although only ten when she died, was quite a pretty child'

Silence followed as thoughts they all didn't want to have to address crowded in.

Ernest broke the impasse. 'I'm not implying anything; just another unturned stone; now overturned.' He felt the charged air in the room that they were all experiencing, 'and,' he hadn't finished yet. 'I went to visit Bill Wilson as you know, and I also learned a thing or two from him.'

They all waited, totally intent on catching every word, as Ernest continued. 'Wilson informed me that young Chris Knowles, used to borrow his binoculars to bird watch; seems old Bill was quite fond of the lad.'

'Dirty old man,' uttered Lisa again.

'Yes, and we know the professor is gay; preferring males to females, but in those days remember it was still kept under wraps. Anyway I digress.' Ernest took a breath before continuing. 'The question is did young Chris see anything he shouldn't, and did he tell anyone . . . . Food for thought surely, and more investigation needed. I felt that Chris Knowles knew much more than he would admit too.'

Jiten spoke up again. 'How old was Chris when his sister was killed?'

'About twelve, just about the age when hormones start to show themselves.' replied Ernest. Jiten's head went down, as he scribbled something in his notebook.

Jack brought up the subject of the fracture on the skull; and that started a whole new train of thought.

'What do you think sir?' Again Lisa reinforced the title Jack had used earlier to address Ernest; to confirm that Ernest had the experience and was very much in charge.

Ernest responded with honesty, after thinking about what his brother had claimed the night before. 'Dr. Radcliffe wasn't the brightest button in the box towards the end, he was in his sixties at the time; early sixties that is, and he developed Alzheimer's disease. We, that is myself and others, thought that we could have asked for a second opinion, but again it all ceased when the investigations were stopped and any verdict left pending.'

'Good God, sir.' Jiten exploded; his sense of fair play disillusioned. 'Do you mean there could have been a cover up?'

Lisa snorted, making it clear she didn't think someone that wasn't of her religion should use such offending language.

Jiten picked it up. 'Same God luv, and I did say good.' She glared at him and muttered something about not taking the Lord's name in vain.

Ernest sighed. 'Alright, let's get on with it. Jack, I want you to pick up more gossip about the late detective chief inspector, especially about his younger years as a detective inspector, and . . . ,' he stopped, obviously contemplating something else, before adding; 'his brother Mike. Were they close? and . . . .' Ernest hadn't finished yet. 'Jiten, I want you to find out if there was any scandal about the prof. and young boys?'

Ernest turned and looked hard and long at the photograph of Jennie Knowles, then turned to his team and patting his chest, added, 'I feel we are onto something.'

Taking a long breath, and for the first time exposing his past vulnerability; now determined to put the record straight. 'Every stone, it's up to us to look under them all, for I'm certain the answer is staring us in the face.'

After the talk, there seemed to be a fire lit under them. It drove new energy into the team and as Ernest left the small room, he sensed the vibrations. Making his way to the upper floor, he found someone who was able to give him the telephone number of the profiler that had helped Lisa in her last case.

He phoned the number and got through to a pleasant voice right away. He talked and the profiler listened; before a time and place was set for a meeting.

Chapter 28

The room was cold; a damp cold that sends shivers through the body and no amount of extra clothes seemed unable to keep it out. Lisa felt it all morning, from waking up, to driving to the police headquarters in spite of wearing a thick cardigan.

She tapped the iron radiator in the cold-case room, expecting it to be hot as it usually was, but someone had forgotten to turn it on. Opening the radiator valve, she waited a while for it to warm up before leaning her buttock against it.

The warmth spread, she sighed, turned and warmed the front part of her body. So involved with wriggling around to enjoy the moment of warmth, she didn't hear the door opening.

'Lucky radiator,' the voice laughed as she spun around to face the blue eyes of Tony Arbury winking at her.

'Bloody hell Arbury,' she straightened up glaring at the police profiler. 'Don't ever creep up on me again like that.'

'Sorry, should have knocked.' He still stood, just looking at her, before dropping his gaze and casing out the room. 'A bit claustrophobic isn't it?' he asked after a while.

'Suits us just fine,' replied Lisa, hating the slightest criticism of her work place, 'better by far than being at home with no one to talk to.'

Tony seemed to understand immediately and tried another tack.

'Well being back in the saddle certainly suits you.'

That didn't seem to work either as she scowled back. If Tony had any doubts at all about his success as a profiler, he might have looked again at Lisa's personality. There had been times he'd felt himself getting close; then abruptly shut out again, however she was an interesting case worth pursuing.

Lisa was now studying him, aware that her buttocks were getting quite hot; but not willing to move.

'So what's your motive here,' she challenged him. 'Analysing us all or just looking for one bad apple.'

He knew she was referring to herself, and to the fact that she had never called for backup a few months ago; putting her comrades in danger.

Tony crossed the room, looked at her for a second before hoisting himself up on top of the side of the desk; hands clasped together.

'No Lisa, I thought you very brave and so did many others; rules are just rules and sometimes cause a hiccup in our life.' He crossed his legs as if he was there to stay. 'I'm here to help Detective Inspector Heath to find out a little more about the personalities he's interviewed.'

Lisa liked the reference to Ernest; there was no retirement mentioned; just an acknowledgement he was up to the job.

At that moment, Ernest threw the door open and came striding across the room.

'Arbury, good lad, you've made it,' he shivered, chilled to the marrow. The English weather doesn't half change; yesterday beautiful and now. He didn't finish or need to, as Jiten followed him in rubbing his own hands too.

'All here?' Ernest asked as he looked around. Lisa offered the name 'Jack', but that seemed to be dismissed as not too important.

'OK, let's get on.' Ernest spoke quickly; he had a lot of questions.

'First, Tony Arbury here is a profiler and I know you all know what that means, but just in case its not quite clear, Tony can, nine out of ten times, tell you how a person will act over a situation, drawing on his knowledge about a person's past.'

Ernest's eyes searched the room.

'Scary, isn't it?' he added.

Stepping forward; Tony coughed and cleared his throat.

'Not quite as the gov. says, but very near it. Now I have here a list of people involved in the cold case and have read their reports; so who goes first.'

'Let's start with the mother and father of Jennie Knowles,' Lisa suggested. 'After all, they were the closest to her.'

Tony suggested the report was interesting; but not bringing anything unusual to the table. Anger, sorrow, disbelief, depression are all normal emotions of parents losing a child in such a dreadful way.

'And Bill Wilson, what can you come up with about him?' asked Ernest, sitting back with his arms folded behind his head.

The profiler thought for a moment. 'Probably a little excited to know some sort of ritual took place again after thousands of years. Yes, I'd say it stimulated him, although knowing the girl, it would give him a sense of guilt too.'

Lisa was fidgeting, frustrated at Arbury's synopsis. He was telling them nothing more than the average person in the street could have done.

'Maise Knowles?' The occupants of the room stared at the speaker wondering where he was going as he was talking about the late detective chief inspector's wife.

'Maise probably knew her husband married her to take him up the ladder of his profession. She must have known about his reputation for liking pretty young women, and by all accounts I've heard about Maise; her looks and age, she was certainly not in that group. So I would say you could be looking at jealousy, anger, hurt; and capable of going out on a limb if pushed far enough.'

There was an intake of breath and suddenly Lisa was looking at him with renewed respect.

'Do you think . . . ,' Jiten broke in, and then looked down at his notes in confusion as he became the centre of attention.

The profiler sighed. 'Not my job to wrap up the case, all I'm telling you is how people would feel, and maybe act, but even that should not be taken literally.'

His eyes locked with Lisa's and her face suddenly reddened.

He continued; half smiling at her discomfort. 'Now the persons I would like to know more about are the professor and Christopher Knowles, but having said that, it is always hard to pin-point the behaviour of someone like Bill Wilson.' He stopped momentarily, considering the right way of expressing his thoughts.

'We know Bill likes his own kind. Nothing wrong in that, the human chemistry doesn't always follow the code we humans have laid down.'

'Nice way of putting it.' Ernest chipped in. The late-comer to the meeting Jack Buzzard nodded; appearing unfazed by the conversation. 'But it does sometimes put others at risk if it's involving minors,' the profiler added.

'Like young Chris you mean.' Jiten asked.

Tony nodded again. 'Might be Chris experienced something, and if he did, it could affect him in many ways. Helplessness that could result in control, even revulsion of the sex act itself; or he may have just got on with his life. Who knows, we all act differently.'

Lisa was looking at the floor, thinking that after all of Arbury's analysing, he hadn't told them a dam thing that she hadn't already considered. She squirmed in her chair a little; as his voice droned on.

'What I suggest is that you discreetly check why Bill Wilson retired early from Oxford University.' Arbury looked down at his notes before adding. 'Maybe talk to some of his students that had visited him in Gelsby around the time Jennie Knowles was killed.'

Hope seeped though Ernest's veins and even Lisa sat up straight to catch what was coming next.

'I strongly recommend you check the whereabouts of Christopher Knowles after he went to Australia, and if there was anything that had brought him to the attention of the police there?'

Chapter 29

There was a buss around the police headquarters that spoke of the Cold Case Team being onto something. It hadn't gone unnoticed that the four of them that huddled in the canteen corner table, were animated and talked in whispers, closing ranks if anyone tried to join them. To those in the department, it was a familiar pattern, a trail had been scented and they were anxious to seek out the quarry.

Detective Inspector Doug Phillips sensed it, and passed his observations on to the detective chief inspector, who then mentioned it to the detective superintendant. Half an hour later Ernest was called to the superintendant's office.

Ernest sat down in the armchair the super indicated; knowing full well the methods used to make one feel comfortable. First the superintendant tried the friendly approach, asking how everything was going and if the cold case team had everything they needed, trying to establish some sort of empathy and friendship between them. Ernest had been there; done that many times. Coffee next he thought. Two minutes later the super's secretary came in carrying a tray.

'So Heath, what have you got for me?' The superintendant asked; one hand tapped the other; as he leaned forward to hear some good news that could only add to his own achievements.

Ernest pursed his lips, secretly enjoying the Super's anticipation that he would open up and spill out all he had. However, what came out was obviously a great disappointment to the big man, as Ernest shrugged his shoulders nonchalantly.

'Not much but getting there,' replied Ernest; offering a small shit-sandwich to keep the interest going. 'Still interviewing all the people involved in some way. PC Buzzard is fishing for gossip as he;' Ernest stopped; as the superintendant waved his hand.

'Good. Buzzard's good at smelling out that sort of thing; he's known most of the locals since a boy.'

Ernest nodded. The superintendant waited; sat back and fiddled with his pencil. Ernest watched; dots made by the pencil getting blacker, as it was pounded on some note paper. 'You had Tony Arbury with you earlier I hear.'

Ernest nodded, thinking it was a bloody small world, when word got around so fast, but no one was going to close it down around his ears again. He'd waited too long. He found himself being eyed over and evaluated. Whatever the outcome of this conversation; it seemed he was going to be allowed to continue.

'I'll give you more time then, and I'll do everything I can to keep the coppers rolling.' He stopped abruptly at a laugh that came from Ernest, who remarked, 'coppers rolling, sir!'

'Quite so,' the super managed a half smile, and then made some reference to the Jennie Knowles investigation that had never been resolved.

Ernest brooded about the meeting with the super for the rest of the morning and afternoon, certain that he was really referring to the late Detective Chief Inspector Knowles' report. Why . . . ? It was that question that made him resolve to give Betty Knowles another visit in the near future.

After he had left the superintendent's office, there was a message for him from Lisa, telling him, she'd tried to get hold of him all morning and it was time he got himself a cell phone. Ernest scowled, if the younger generation knew how silly they looked with their heads bent to one side; hand over the ear and half the time oblivious to where they were walking.

He sighed, stared at the silent computer and knew why people retire. The older they got the quicker things seemed to change at a very fast pace. He idly ran his fingers over the keyboard, remembering his attempts at typing. He looked again at the computer and sat on the chair opposite fiddling with the mouse. Suddenly the whole thing came to life. He pressed one of the buttons on the mouse and was confronted again with more instructions. Pulling his chair closer, he put on his spectacles and started to investigate.

The door opened and the cleaner came in, armed with a vacuum cleaner. Ernest gazed at the intruder over his glasses, and she backed out quickly.

He played around for a little while and when it became a little more complicated he attempted to switch the computer off, which was just as complicated, so he pulled the plug from the wall socket, having no qualms in letting the cleaning lady take the blame.

He was too uptight to go home, and wasn't in the mood to make idle conversation with Roger about the history of the town.

Ernest gazed forlornly around the room. The four walls seemed to have become closer till he realised the light was fading. His eyes sought the clipboard, resting on the name of Chris Knowles. He picked up the phone and dialled.

'Come on lass, pick the damned thing up,' he muttered, visualising Lisa taking her time, thinking it was one of those salesman that knew dinner time was the best time to catch people at home.

Eventually he heard the click of the receiver being lifted.

'Yes.' Her tone was short and a little annoyed. There had been times when feeling tired, she had simply answered, 'City Morgue'

Ernest picked up her tone right away and softened his response. 'It's me.' Again never giving a thought to say who was ringing. However it didn't matter, they both knew.

'What did you get from Australia?'

'Not much as yet gov, but did find out he lived in Sidney, and;' she waited like a prima donna for the applause. 'He has been interviewed by the police there, but nothing came of it.'

'What?' Ernest swivelled the chair around and bent forward; the phone pressed hard to the side of his head.

'They said they would do a little more digging and get back to me.'

Ernest thanked her, knowing there wasn't much hope of further information at that moment, given the time zone difference. He replaced the phone, got up and stood in front of the clip board. He felt something didn't quite sit right when he'd called at the Knowles home the first time, but had dismissed it as Chris was only a young lad at the time of his sister's death. He stood back leaning against the desk, before picking up the marker crayon and adding twelve years old, and stood back again analysing his own gut feelings about him.

The blonde hair and certain features had no resemblance to his father Mike Knowles, but certainly looked a hell of a lot like his one time superior officer.

Ernest asked himself; could Chris Knowles be the late detective chief inspector's son, and then considered all the implications that went along with it.

The interview with Bill Wilson, and his subtle remarks about seeing the detective inspector's car often at the Knowles house, hadn't seemed out of the ordinary, considering the detective inspector's brother lived there. However the more he thought about it, the more he remembered that Mike Knowles would have worked an eight hour day. Too many questions leapt forward to get his head around as he knew he was still emotionally involved, and all the frustration he felt when the case had been wrapped up for lack of evidence.

'What had the late detective chief inspector been hiding?' he asked himself.

Suddenly he felt very tired, so he picked up his coat, switched off the light and drove home. Tomorrow was another day. The Australian Police would have more in the offing, and he had made up his mind to visit Maise Knowles; wife of the late detective chief inspector.

Chapter 30

'Getting anywhere luv?' Rita looked at her husband over the rim of her tea cup.

Head lying back in his comfortable armchair, he was gazing at the ceiling. He grunted something quite unintelligible that prompted his wife to enquire whether he'd like a couple of rounds of burnt toast. He nodded.

Rita sighed, and gave up. She surveyed him out of the corner of her eye. Never in a million years would she have guessed the very lad whose attention span lasted less than two minutes to the frustration of their teacher, would become so one pointed. A wave of affection swept through her as she pushed herself up. She ruffled his thinning hair as she passed him.

Ernest gave a little contented smile, and then reverted to the boxes in his subconscious. Some were placed in a corner and would probably remain there, whilst a few loomed large and opened. The one that kept moving to the front was labelled Maise Knowles.

He thought of Lisa, maybe she should visit her; not so threatening as a male. Then he perished the thought as Lisa's scowling face came to mind.

Suddenly ready for action, Ernest got up and found the telephone directory, which he thumbed through; looking for the name he wanted. He was surprised to find there were nine listed under Knowles, and then recalled that it was a Danesbury family and there would be other offsprings.

The seventh down the list was what he was looking for. He looked at the address, 39 Nelson St.

Ernest knew it, one of the roads near his old school, surprising him a little, as he remembered the late detective chief inspector used to live in a posh area. He made a mental note of the number, calling out to his wife as he slipped on his jacket. 'I'll be back later Rita.' The front door slammed behind him.

Driving; Ernest contemplated Maise's age, wondering if it was the same as her late husband's. He came up with about sixty six, give or take a couple of years, then wondered about her health; the latter thought making him a little uncomfortable at having to bring up the past.

He turned sharply to the left, knowing the old roads like the back of his hand, or so he thought. Horns blasted and windows opened, with one driver shaking his fist. To his horror he had turned into a one way street.

Cursing, he did a u-turn, realising he hadn't a clue which other street would bring him to his destination.

'Why can't they leave well alone,' he muttered angrily. Eventually he found his way to Nelson St. and was surprised to find semi-detached houses where once terraced houses had stood.

Shows how long ago since I was last around here; he recalled the gitty and alleyways, that always provided a good getaway when needed as a lad.

Number thirty nine was a mid-nineteen sixties house in design; brick built and square, with a long flat roof over the front door and a large fluted glass window to the side of it. A small driveway, garage attached to the house with a narrow path providing access to the rear.

He rang the door bell, waited awhile, then pushed it again, holding it in a little longer.

The door opened. He guessed it was Maise Knowles, but would have had a hard time recognising her elsewhere.

She seemed to have shrunk at least an inch or two in height from when he'd last seen her, then he realised her shoulders were so rounded that her head stuck out like tortoise, arthritis had done it's worst on the skeleton frame.

She had to raise her eyes upwards, as her head didn't move. She held a walking stick in her hand which was trembling. Her voice however was surprisingly strong as she surveyed him. 'Come on in then lad and don't just stand there gorping.' He smiled at her Danesbury dialect, as he hadn't heard the word gorping since his grandmother was alive.

'So you recognise me do you; even after all these years.'

'Aye,' she answered as he followed her down the well-carpeted hallway, nearly falling over her as she stopped abruptly; pointing her stick to the room she intended him to go into.

He waited awhile, thinking she'd gone to put the kettle on, but she came back empty handed, shuffling past him to reach the sideboard, where she bent down to open the door on it. She got up; a bottle of whisky under her arm.

'Had to let the damned cat out,' she offered, explaining why she'd left him alone. 'Now how about you getting a couple of glasses from the back of this cupboard here.'

Ernest obeyed automatically, letting the thought of drinking and driving slip, as he poured himself a generous helping. It was a good single malt.

She was the first to speak, after they'd settled down.

'It's about young Jennie, isn't it?'

He nodded. Her hand shook a little as she placed the glass beside her and folded her hands on her lap.

'She was a pretty child; I suppose that was part of the trouble.' Ernest glimpsed at her, he wasn't ready for such honesty to be so forthcoming. 'Alan went at fifty six,' she sighed, 'but you already know that don't you.'

Ernest inclined his head, trying to look sympathetic. 'Yes, I'm sorry.'

'Now don't be sorry lad, my real heart ache ended then.' She took a deep breath, looked at her glass and drained the liquid; before holding out her glass for a refill.

Ernest did the honours, satisfied that Maise was ready to talk; he felt free to push for answers.

'Alan was having an affair with his brother's wife Betty; wasn't he Maise?'

Their eyes locked.

'Aye, never thought it would last as she grew older,' her thoughts were in the past; 'liked young girls you see, always did.' Maise's face seemed to crumble and her eyes filled with tears. 'I loved him,' she stated. 'You remember him, tall, handsome, charming; we all fell for him.' Ernest knew she was referring to her younger years.

'He was a charmer alright.' She took another sip, wiping her mouth on the back of her hand, as the liquid dribbled out of the corner of her mouth. 'Christopher is his child, you know,' she sighed; 'but you knew that didn't you, just by looking at him.' A bitterness edged her voice. 'Like father, like son.'

Ernest felt as if Tony Aubrey was sitting by him explaining that Maise was just emptying out all the dark corners of her mind, so that she could face the rest of her life. Maise hadn't finished.

'I couldn't have children.' There was a little bitterness attached to her confession. 'Mike, his brother was nice enough, although a little on the simple side. I guess that's not a nice word to use these days. Let's say he was slow at not knowing what was going on. He liked his booze you see, and Alan saw he didn't go short.' She paused, before adding, 'you know why he married me, everyone at the police headquarters did. I may not have been a catch, but my father was.'

Ernest didn't respond; instead asked, 'did you ever approach Betty Knowles?' Suddenly, she looked even more frail and vulnerable.

'Another?' queried Ernest; as she offered her glass again; Ernest joined her, this time only adding water to his still unfinished drink.

'The day Jennie was killed.' Her voice was almost too quiet to be heard, and Ernest had to lean forward to catch the rest. 'I went to see Betty to plead with her to leave my husband alone, but . . . .'

'Go on,' he encouraged.

'His car was there,' she said. Ernest sat up; all his attention now focussed on her every word.

'Alan was there or somewhere around, because I saw his car. I didn't know what to do and panicked. I'm not very good at confrontations you see.'

'So you left and went home?'

Silence; followed by a long drawn-out sigh before Maise added. 'No, I reversed and parked my car in someone's driveway.' Bill Wilson's no doubt thought Ernest.

'I came back along the other side of the wall, thinking I might see something, and I did. I saw Alan and Jennie walking up Edge Lane towards the style and the path that goes to the Maidenstone. I was about to follow them when Betty came out, leaning over her garden gate, which seemed for ages; and then she followed them.'

'What!' Ernest sat bolt upright and stared at her.

'Yes, she followed them and I thought if there was going to be any trouble I didn't want to be there, so I went home.'

Ernest sat stunned. All this put new life on the last moments of Jennie's life. He needed to think, iron out the wrinkles as it were. He thanked her and got up to leave.

'Pretty children,' she said with a tinge of regret, 'looked so much like their father.'

Chapter 31

The sky had turned dark threatening a downpour. Ernest let the front room curtains fall back into place. Not the sort of weather for what he had in mind, but then he wasn't in the mood to await a better one.

He left Rita explaining to Roger why she was glad to be back in England, after hearing from a friend in Canada that Toronto was having the worst snowstorm in years.

Roger agreeing that no one could rely on better weather in Canada until May. Ernest mumbled to himself, 'then don't cast a clout, till May be out.'

Rita could have told him that the differences were digging oneself out of six foot snowdrifts, snow tyres on cars, crampons on the boots, not to mention thermal underwear. However the lecture would have been lost on Ernest as his mind was on the job at hand. He slipped the morning paper inside his coat, patted it and opened the door. A tinge of guilt surfaced for about a tenth of a second and was gone.

A sudden downpour hit as he pulled into the parking ground of the police headquarters. The paper was quickly pulled out of his coat, opened and placed as a cover over his head. The police constable at the desk took one look at the apparition and handed over a trash basket. The others must have got there before the downpour as their faces indicated they weren't impressed by his shaking of the dripping coat.

Lisa shook the papers she'd just taken out of the printer and glared as he entered the cold case room.

None of this seemed to rub off on Ernest as he looked around the room, wondering if all the team was present. They were.

'Right, we have work to do, and if I'm not mistaken, we might well be at the end of our trail.'

Jack stopped filing his nails, Jiten had jerked up from reading a fax and Lisa's mouth dropped open; waiting.

Ernest sat on the edge of Lisa's table, where he had a view of all of them.

'So we have to bait the rabbit out of the hole.' He stopped, pausing as he considered voicing his theory; then held back. He didn't want to make any mistakes this time.

Stretching his arms and placing his hands behind his head. 'Lisa, you and I are going to pay Betty Knowles a visit. Jiten, I want you to follow in your car but to stop out of sight of the Knowles house. Maybe at the crossroads would be the best place.' He caught the look on Jack's face, as he expected to hear that he was being passed over as usual.

'Jack, I want you to visit the prof. Let him know that we are making enquiries, and make sure he doesn't leave the cottage.'

Jiten raised a hand, 'why am I to stay at the crossroads sir?'

'I want you close by; in case needed.'

Lisa's face broke into a smile. 'So gov. you've got Christopher Knowles tied up, after that report came in from Australia. You can't blame yourself. Who would have suspected him being a pimp to under-aged girls?'

She was on a roll and the words came tumbling out. 'No wonder the detective chief inspector closed the books; him being the father and all.' She considered the relationship even further. 'I guess that made the superintendant, Chris' grandfather.'

The storm was in for the day; humid air from the coast hitting the Welsh mountains before crossing the Cheshire plains and releasing its load.

The thunder clouds were still above them when the two cars drove to Edge Lane; flashes of lightning streaked through the heavens, leaving Ernest wondering if the old gods knew of their mission.

They left Jiten with a car at the cross roads and stopped by the prof's gate; Jack looking totally dejected when Ernest refused to drive him up the muddy lane.

Ernest drove on, and the first thing he noticed was the blue Accord, as they pulled up outside the house. Ernest looked at Lisa and nodded. They got out at the same time and made for the front door, both squeezing in a little as they tried to shelter under the porch roof.

Chris opened the front door; looked at them warily, summed up Lisa, and then stood aside to let them enter.

His mother Betty was standing in the kitchen doorway; her eyes resembling some hunted animal, as they flicked from them to her son.

'I think you'd both better take those off,' suggested Chris; gazing down at their wet, muddy shoes.

Chris stood over them with a condescending look, which made Ernest think that Tony Aubury would have had an opinion about investigators, kneeling at the feet of those being investigated.

To correct the balance, both Ernest and Lisa insisted on standing when taken into the front room. It was Betty who spoke first. 'Have you arrested the person that killed Anna Booth?'

The name put Ernest off his stride. It hadn't dawned on him that they thought he was here because of the recent death. He eyed her for a second before answering.

'No Betty, I'm here to ask you a few questions, and it's up to you whether you want your son present or not. You see I've been talking to Maise Knowles.'

Betty gave a long sigh; glanced at Chris and then at Ernest, before adding; 'Chris knows he's also Alan's son. It doesn't take a rocket scientist to see the resemblance, now does it.'

Ernest glanced at Christopher who was leaning against the wall; his supercilious smile confirming his mother's confession, but Ernest hadn't finished. 'And Jennie . . . . ; she was Alan's too, wasn't she?'

This time the response was slower and her face paled, as she kept it diverted from her son's.

Ernest's voice became softer. He leaned forward towards the elderly woman, his hands interlocked.

'Alan used to take Jennie for walks, didn't he?' Chris uttered something; as he prepared himself to defend his mother.

Ernest ignored it and he continued slowly and deliberately, knowing that Lisa was fully prepared for any action.

'Alan Knowles liked young girls Betty; it was common knowledge when he was younger.' He paused. 'How old were you luv, when he got inside your pants?'

Betty stared at him. Chris growled and attempted to move forward, but Lisa's arm restrained him.

Ernest's voice was quiet, but his eyes never left Betty's face as he continued. 'He took Jennie for a walk the day she was killed, didn't he? And you followed them.'

There was a slight whimper; then deadly silence. Even Chris seemed to have shrunk back against the wall; afraid of what he was about to hear.

Lisa's eyes were glued on Ernest's face. She was beginning to get confused.

'Betty,' exclaimed Ernest, as he reached out and took hold of the small trembling hand. 'I think I know what happened all those years ago, when Maise told me she had seen you following them; it all fell into place.'

'I don't know exactly what it was you saw, but I imagine it was the end of the line for you. After all those years of loving someone who had palmed you off on his brother, having to listen to village gossip about his deviations; and then having two children by him. It would have been enough for most women I dare say. But then Alan Knowles overstepped the line you could not accept.'

Betty had a vacant look about her now. She'd stopped listening and was staring at the photograph of her daughter. Then she spoke in quiet voice.

'I made a mistake. I should have thrown the rock at him, not her, but she laughed at me.'

Lisa wanted to cough but it got stuck. Chris' breathing became heavy, as if he was struggling with his own demons. His foot began to tap on the floor; he was becoming very agitated and Lisa wished Ernest would get on with it.

'You threw the rock that killed your daughter, didn't you Betty?'

Betty winced, the memory flooding back. 'It was an accident, I was angry. I didn't mean to kill her.'

Half an hour later, police backup had been called and a broken woman was led out of the house.

Chapter 32

It was a day for celebration, and the Cold Case Team was centre stage. When the four of them walked down the aisle separating the two rows of desks, a cheer went up and hands clapped them on their backs.

It was slightly more sober in the superintendant's office. It was the first time any of them had seen him look so tired, and Ernest guessed why. He was aware the police department would suffer at the hands of the press, when the full story came out. However, he also knew from experience that the late Detective Chief Inspector Knowles' name would be kept out of it.

Betty Knowles had suffered a major stroke after being brought in for questioning and there was no way she was fit enough to stand trial. The verdict would, no doubt, be accidental death. After all, it was a long time ago and the recent murder was the one that worried the locals.

All this hardly mattered to Ernest; he had achieved his life long ambition to bring every case he was involved in to a conclusive end. The other members of the team benefitted in various ways. Detective Sergeant Pharies was brought back to work on the recent homicide immediately. Detective Constable Smith was to be sent on a course to further his career and Police Sergeant Buzzard had the best retirement party that had ever been put on.

To celebrate further, Rita had arranged a table at the Horseshoe for them all, offering to pay whatever it cost, saying it would be worth it to get her husband back.

It turned out to be a pleasant evening when they got together.

By 5.30 pm, they had all arrived. Rita felt pleased she had booked early before the locals came in. Two tables had been placed together by the window. Rita had insisted on a tablecloth that put the new bartender into panic; until he remembered he still had one they used for wedding receptions.

Lisa slid along the bench by the window and Rita stepped aside to let Jiten in, giving Lisa a little smile, which was ignored. Jack managed to command the carver chair with its padded seat. Roger graciously pulled out a chair for Rita and settled her in, receiving a frown from his brother, who had already made certain it was he who was going to sit by his wife.

The log fire had been lit, it wasn't often the Horseshoe did it these days, but as long as the free pile of logs lasted they were used. Sometimes the landlord wished the farmers would keep their wood to themselves, having secret visions of a nice reproduction gas fire in its place, but the locals didn't like change.

The meal offered was well worth the expense. It included fresh river trout, wild rice and two veg; with a large lemon meringue pie for afters.

Good wine, great company, Rita sat back well satisfied; although she knew a flood of questions needing answers would also be forthcoming.

She was right as usual, and it was Jiten who was the one to open the topic by addressing Ernest. 'What I fail to understand was why Jack was sent to visit the prof.?'

Ernest gazed at him after taking a sip of his wine. 'Just a few things I wanted to know about the past and I thought Jack here; the right man for the job. He would know if the prof was a two sided coin, so to speak.'

All heads turned to look at Jack, who was totally unfazed by the comment, and just went on helping himself to the last piece of pie. Suddenly Lisa kicked Jiten under the table and made a face at him. Jiten quickly picked up on the fact that the prof and Jack Buzzard were both gay and was probably behind Ernest's reason for choosing Jack for that interview, he might pick something up.

Jack sat back wiping his lips, quite unabashed at his the mission and cleared the air willingly. 'No, I'm certain he was not interested in the female species and no, I'm also certain there was no relationship between Bill Wilson and Chris. In fact, Bill Wilson got quite upset and gave me a mouthful about suggesting such a thing. Right he was too . . . , he did tell me one thing though; he suspected Chris used his binoculars for more than bird watching.'

'What was he looking for then?' demanded Lisa.

Five pair of eyes turned to stare at her. It was Rita who broke the silence.

'Really Lisa, what the hell do you think he watched?' The Edge is a great place for couples who want a little privacy.'

Lisa's face coloured quickly from embarrassment, as Ernest stepped in quickly.

'I wanted to know a little more about Chris, although I'd already eliminated him from Jennie's death. It was the Australian report that made me think what our profiler would have made of a peeping-tom getting turned on by watching couples.'

'Then he had nothing to do with his sister's death,' said Lisa looking frustrated.

'Sorry love.' Ernest looked apologetic. 'I'm walking two separate paths here, so I'd better come clean.'

Roger poured everyone another drink and held up his hand to the waiter for a couple more bottles; while his brother continued talking.

'I'd already made up my mind as to who killed Jennie and it was Roger here who set me on the right track, after saying the angle of the fracture was not caused by a close blow to the head.'

Roger nodded as Ernest continued. 'So I rightfully assumed that the rock had been thrown and I admit Chris entered my mind, but then after a little checking with Maise Knowles who told me that after she'd driven to the Edge to confront Betty; she saw her husband's car there. She waited awhile and witnessed young Chris with his fishing tackle, going down the hill towards the river before Alan and Jennie came out; followed after awhile by Betty, and it was at this point I eliminated Chris.'

Lisa waited a few seconds for Ernest to take a sip of his wine, and then asked. 'Couldn't Alan Knowles have thrown the stone?'

With all eyes now on Lisa, Ernest was somewhat taken aback by her question.

'Yes Lisa, it had crossed my mind also, but why would Alan want to kill her; the autopsy said Jennie wasn't interfered with, and remember Betty, her mother, knew they were out together. I don't think her loyalty would have extended to covering up for him if he had killed her daughter. It's much more likely she found him trying to kiss or cuddle the child. Perhaps Betty, in anger, threw a stone that unfortunately killed her.'

'But that's all presumption. No evidence or proof.' Jiten added; looking concerned and uncertain.

'Right you are Jiten, but sometimes you have to pretend you have all the facts and try your theory out, and in my case Betty Knowles confessed all.'

'But what the hell was I doing waiting in a police car at the crossroads.' It had been bugging Jiten all along.

'Oh, that was in case I had it wrong, and maybe someone might try making a run for it.'

It seemed to satisfy Jiten; although Lisa had a sneaking suspicion that Ernest didn't really know what to do with a young detective constable.

Lisa hadn't finished. 'So the late detective chief inspector covered it all up; fearing for his reputation in case Betty confessed, even though it had been an accident.'

There was silence around the table, until Roger raised his glass.

'To the Cold Case Team . . . . Congratulations.'

They all raised their glasses, clicking them together, before Roger spoke again. 'Well folks, it's been a great experience meeting you all, and of course finding my brother and his charming wife. Sad to say, much as I've enjoyed every minute here, I need to get back to my own home.'

Ernest gazed at him. He had a hard job explaining the feeling that overwhelmed him at that moment. Rita understood; for he felt her hand on his knee.

'Well I'll miss you big bro,' said Ernest, while offering his hand across the table which was clasped tightly. 'We would have made a great team,' referring to Roger's medical observations.

Roger smiled. 'Don't know who we got it from.'

Ernest laughed. 'Gran was a smart old thing you know.'

Lisa was fidgeting tapping her fingers on the table, suddenly realising however, she had everyone's attention. 'Well,' she said stiffly. 'It's all very well solving a case thirty years old, but what about the poor girl that was murdered at the same place not so long ago.'

Ernest looked up. 'Lisa, that's for you to solve now that you're back on the job. But there are a number suspects I would look into. I will give you something to think about later.'

Before Lisa could answer, there appeared a smiling Frank Butterworth at their table. Addressing Ernest, he said. 'There's a meeting Thursday night at the Parish Hall. Hope you've decided to join us.'

To everyone's surprise, including his own, Ernest answered.

'Right, I'll be there.'

Rita momentarily wondered if the amount of wine he'd drunk had anything to do with his response.

Chapter 33

Ernest felt a small warm hand slip into his as he and his wife waved Roger goodbye. They stood for a while watching the car disappear slowly around the corner.

'He'll be back luv.' His wife said with conviction and Ernest knew she was right, but still a little piece of him felt abandoned.

He shivered, the evenings were closing in, and the damp air seemed to go through one's very bones.

'Come on Ernest.' Rita insisted; shivering herself as she wrapped her cardigan closer around her chest. 'I think there's a good film on the telly later, it will be nice to relax together once again.'

Ernest bit on his bottom lip, finding it hard to contain the emotions that all day had been flooding through him and hadn't yet been resolved. 'Get it done,' he then told himself. Once he'd finished the job in hand; only then could he relax.

'Ah luv,' he sighed with the realization of having to do something first; when he'd rather be watching telly with his wife.

Rita glanced up, after slipping off her shoes. The look she gave him said what now; but all she did was sigh.

'I sort of mentioned to Lisa I'd slip over for half an hour.' Ernest waited for a response, and when nothing was said, he carried on. 'The lass has just been reinstated luv; and I think I can help her.'

He failed to see his wife's half smile; she already knew he had something up his sleeve. Boy or man, some things never change; when it came to the bond that had always held them together.

Suddenly Rita laughed. 'Go on then get whatever it is off your chest, especially if she can benefit from it, better get it out of your system before the parish council needs your services, eh!'

Two minutes later, Lisa was stepping aside to allow Ernest to enter number seven.

'Cuppa tea,' she asked him.

Ernest was quick to refuse as Lisa's milk was not always as fresh as it should be. 'I could handle a small whisky though;' demonstrating the shot-glass mark with his finger.

Ernest sat down and stretched out his long legs before crossing them. Two hands cupping his glass, he glanced at the ram-rod straight figure in the chair opposite.

'So lass, you're back on the job then.' He raised his glass to celebrate the occasion, a gesture she seemed to ignore.

'Any ideas about the case you'll be working on?' he asked; leaning forward.

Lisa's hands shook a little, she appeared stressed, and Ernest understood. First there was the stigma of the investigation and her suspension from the last case she was on; not to mention the convicted murderer was her boyfriend at the time. Second, with the injury she'd received, although now healed, a lot of her confidence had been lost.

Working alongside Ernest and her friends on the Cold Case Team was one thing, but being put back onto another more recent case was something else. 'What if I mess that up too?' It was a question she'd been asking herself following her reinstatement in the force.

Lisa looked at her old boss, and wished so hard things were as they once were. It was a good team and she respected the retired detective inspector so much.

A tear ran slowly down her cheek and she sniffed, wiping the back of her hand to clear it. Her black mascara smudged and left a dark mark; making her eye slightly blackened.

Ernest smiled, first at the way she looked, but more secretly at what he had to tell her. He took a sip of the golden liquid, feeling its warmth run down his throat, before putting down the glass. He leaned forward, his hands locked together and his eyes focussed on the person in front of him.

'Lisa if I were you I'd look into the Professor William Wilson's background a little more.'

Lisa looked puzzled, and then moved forward too, making any conversation between them more intimate. 'Out with it gov,' she demanded; a blush forming on her cheeks.

There was silence for a moment, which to Lisa seemed like an eternity. 'Lisa do you remember during your last case . . . ,' Lisa winced for a moment, but Ernest carried on. 'Remember, Rita and I went to Oxford University to find out more about the man who was murdered in the hotel.'

Lisa's mind leapt back over the past few months and recalled clearly the hotel room where a man was murdered that started the long investigation that followed; leading to her suspension due to her slipshod mistaken heroism. She nodded.

Ernest continued; 'well lass, while we were there talking to a proctor of one of the colleges, he asked about Professor Wilson, and did he still live in Danesbury? We had a little chat, and I learnt something of interest, but was too focussed on the job in hand at the time to let it sink in,' he paused . . . , 'that was until the cold case came up.'

She gave herself a quick shake, trying to recall events of recent cold case investigation Lisa remained silent, her mouth slightly open, before adding with mounting interest. 'Go on gov.'

Ernest smiled, whether it was her tone of voice or something from the past, but he knew he had all her brain cells working overtime and focused. 'It seems,' he looked down, fiddling with a broken nail on his finger. 'It seems,' he repeated again, but this time a little louder, 'that our professor was sacked.' He paused again, 'maybe sacked is the wrong word for being dismissed from a university, but it means the same.'

Lisa's eyes widened, as surge of adrenaline started; it was like he was opening some Pandora's Box.

'Go on, go on,' she urged, 'for what?'

Here Ernest couldn't help himself; he loved the suspense that had driven so many of his colleagues to grip the edge of their chairs.

'I was told by the proctor that the then, much younger Professor William Wilson, was writing some thesis on Neolithic or Bronze Age sacrifices; he wasn't sure which.'

Lisa fidgeted . . . God this guy is so frustrating, get on with it her inner voice kept saying.

Ernest continued, 'well it seems he misused university ethics standards to re-enact a sacrificial ceremony by insisting his students took a drug he had researched as the most likely one used during a Bronze Age period.'

Lisa gasped, 'and what happened?'

'He went too far and actually picked up a stone to hit the girl, who was acting as the sacrificial person, but was stopped in time from maybe hurting her.'

'Golly.' Lisa's eyes grew wider. 'You mean he could have killed her?'

Ernest shrugged. 'Who knows, it was all hushed up, and unfortunately things like that get forgotten as just another experiment into the behaviour of past generations.'

'Some would, I don't,' stated Lisa emphatically.

The room went silent, both deep in their own thoughts; till Lisa jumped up. 'Another?' She asked, nodding at his glass.

'No thanks luv, enough is enough for one day,' as he finished off the rest of his whisky.

'Cuppa then,'

He shook his head and motioned for her to sit down again. 'When I interviewed the prof, I noticed a pair of old binoculars in a leather case with a broken strap.' He stopped for a moment before continuing, 'the same type of leather material as the one you found and brought to us from the Edge during the cold case investigation. I wondered if the prof had maybe witnessed Jennies' death, and if it still held some sort of fascination for him.'

Lisa grinned at him. 'Come on gov, that was thirty years ago, wouldn't you think he would have finished all his drug experiments long before.'

Ernest added, 'same thought went through my mind, until I remembered him saying he'd once thought of writing a book on sacrifices to the gods and considered that this was now the time.'

He stopped, lost in his own thoughts. 'I just thought, lots of us hope to achieve our younger dreams when retired and have the time. Maybe he wanted to do it before he died.'

Lisa sat still pondering the consequences of messing up again, but the scent of catching the fox was too stimulating.

'Right Ernest, I will follow the trail and see if it comes to anything, but . . . ,' she paused, 'no promises mind; but this time it gets to be done by the rules.'

Ernest nodded; satisfied he'd unloaded his suspicions into the right hands. 'Hear you luv, but I'll bet a pound to a dollar, I'm right.'

Lisa half smiling added; 'that must be one of Rita's Canadian expressions surely.'

Chapter 34

Lisa woke up long before her alarm clock went off. For hours it seemed, she had lain awake; staring into the darkness.

Sometimes her over-active mind would race and in her imagination, the course of future events would take over and bring on anxieties. Then there were periods of blankness; just staring into the dark void all around her.

The daylight only brought further anxiety. Instead of the excitement of being recalled to duty; Lisa found herself being lulled by all the weariness of a victim of a sleepless night.

The feeling lingered during the drive to work followed by a slight sickness in her stomach as she entered the police headquarters.

So she was surprised and relieved at the response of the desk sergeant, who had leaned over the counter and held out his hand.

'Welcome back Pharies,' he said with an enthusiastic shake of her limp cold hand. Blushing, she responded with a grateful smile. That wasn't too bad she mused as she walked down the long corridor to the main central area. Hand on the door bar, she took a deep breath and pushed it open, stepping into the room full of desks and computers, some partitioned off by screens, and walls covered with flip boards and notices.

As she stepped through them, a sound of slow hand-clapping started and slowly intensified as she moved forward. Some of them were holding up a long strip of paper.

WELCOME BACK LISA

She'd experienced this display before as she worked on the cold case, but this time she was back among her colleagues, reinstated and one of them once again. Never one for displays of any kind where she was the centre of all the attention, she blushed to a pinkness that any flowering rose would have envied. For a second her injured leg wanted to give way and trembled. Suddenly the room quietened down as the door opened once again; this time framing the large figure of Detective Chief Inspector Granger. A pin could have been heard dropping as his voice bellowed out behind her.

'Pharies, my office: Now.'

Lisa turned, her heart thumping as walked along the corridor to his office.

The detective chief inspector stood behind his desk, eyeing her over and, noting her slight unsteadiness, pointed to a chair.

'Sure your leg's okay?' his voice sounded genuinely concerned. She nodded, and replied, 'as good as normal.'

She'd lied; now aware it was aching.

'Good, good.' He nodded for her to take a seat in front of his desk. 'Feel ready to work full time?'

Lisa nodded again, wondering if he was aware of her recent full days of activity on the cold case, or if he thought she'd just sat at a desk all the time. Her lips formed a thin line, a sign she was slightly irritated.

Still standing he turned his back on her and walked over to the window. Lifting the venetian blind, he peered out; letting it drop again before turning around. He moved back to his desk, but remaining standing.

Suddenly he bent over the desk, his two large hands flat on the top, fingers spread out. Then with a plop, he sank down into the swivel chair.

'Good work on the cold case.' His praise sounded genuine; before leaning back and staring at Lisa, which to her seemed like an eternity.

'Thank you sir,' she managed; but began to fret as to where all this was leading.

Suddenly he hit the top of his desk with the flat of his hand.

'What I want now . . . ,' he stopped for an intake of breath. 'Nay, what I insist on is the solving and finalisation of the Anna Booth case.'

Lisa nodded, but didn't say anything; instinct warning her only to listen, as her superior was too preoccupied by his own thoughts and not her response.

Then he focused his attention back onto her again. 'First Pharies, you will be reinstated to your former position as a detective sergeant, and . . . ,' he eyed her closely as if making up his mind, before adding; 'I've been told by the powers that be, your chances of making detective inspector are good.'

He held up his hand to stop her saying anything, not that she was about to; as her breathing had momentarily stopped.

'Those chances will depend very much on the present case; the Anna Booth case.' The detective chief inspector eyed Lisa to see if there was any reaction. Finding only her intense concentration; he added. 'The Anna Booth case must be solved quickly.' All the preamble of the interview was tied up in that one sentence.

A long sigh escaped and a frown formed on his forehead. Lisa noticed for the first time he was looking older; as grey hairs now competed with the natural brown she remembered. Subconsciously and without knowing why, she reminded herself to check out her own hair colour. Inwardly she wished he'd let her get on with it and let her start working. The figure of Prof. Bill Wilson flashed through her mind.

'The recent case has to be resolved,' the detective chief inspector repeated. 'The town is angry that we still haven't charged anyone.' He paused, took a breath and with emphasis said, 'a young girl murdered, a killer loose; maybe one of their neighbours. Every parent is worried about the safety of their kids.'

The detective chief inspector shook his head. 'The children are taken to school; not allowed to play outside unless in the garden, and escorted everywhere. It's a nightmare I tell you. Folks are getting angry, and where will they throw the blame?' He banged his hand hard on the desk again. 'Right here.'

Lisa sat tight waiting for the pent up anger to subside, she understood all he was saying and the pressure he had to deal with in a town where most people knew each other.

DCI Granger sighed, the floodgates of his own anxiety now released, he turned and indicated with his head to the coffee percolator in the corner. Lisa nodded.

The strong coffee poured and sipped seemed to have broken the cycle and changed the direction of the conversation. She was patiently waiting to find out who she would be working with.

The detective chief inspector was now speaking calmly. 'DC Smith has already been assigned to you, and of course, any one else you may need from the police force for support, within reason.'

Lisa stared at him in surprise; her hands shook just enough to feel a small splash of hot coffee on her hand. She ignored the burn, 'and yourself sir?' Lisa asked; puzzled at no mention of whom she would be reporting to.

Her superior sighed before explaining, things are not as easy at the moment.

'It's the bloody Irish, setting bombs off. It seems there may be a couple of those chaps hiding out in the Danesbury area.' He stopped, letting the implication tell its own story.

Lisa accepted the implication with an understanding nod, for there was an area in the old part of the town where Irish families had settled years before; and still remained.

As a child herself, she remembered the unemployed workers, sometimes a little tipsy, singing on the street corner. Yes it was a possible place for a fellow country-man to hide for awhile; although it sounded a little racial to her.

'So Detective Sergeant Pharies; there you have it,' the detective chief inspector suddenly seemed more relaxed. For the moment you will be reporting directly to me. 'Don't mess up.' Lisa stood up and took hold of the hand offered, and as she turned to go, he added 'I don't care if it's the UK Government's Chief of Police himself; I want the girl's killer, Pharies.'

Lisa half smiled to herself by the reference to the UK's Chief of Police. What her superior was saying was; 'get the job done, and make sure the right person is arrested.'

Oh yes, she would find the killer and had a fairly good idea where to start looking, thanks to her old gov. Her heart was racing, not from anxiety, but with stimulation and the need to start things rolling.

Chapter 35

Although Detective Chief Inspector Granger was officially in charge of the recent homicide, there were some murmurings of resentment when Detective Sergeant Pharies let it be known that she would be very much at the forefront of the investigation.

Aware of this, Lisa took the position, as she always did, to ignore the groups and their facial expressions during coffee breaks. DC Smith, as always her able side-kick; gave his total support to her.

Lisa's first port of call was to interview first hand Anna Booth's parents. She put aside any feelings of guilt at opening up the emotional wounds of the parents; however it did bring a show of resentment from the father, when Lisa asked her first question.

'What was a ten year old doing out on the Edge alone?' The question she asked felt more than fair, as it must have been on most of the townsfolk's minds as they gossiped.

'Good god, woman.' The father offered no respect for the police visit; his face showing all the signs of irritation. 'It's all written down, and I've repeated it over and over again to you lot.' The last two words holding contempt for the police failure to apprehend their daughter's killer.

'I understand, but please bare with me.' Lisa remained focussed and unfazed by the reaction.

But the mother interrupted; her voice wavering with tiredness and grief. 'Our Anna was at her gran's, and seeing the quizzical look of her visitor's faces; she added. 'My mother lives on the Edge.' She stared at the young officer in front of her.

Mrs Booth's hands tightened on her knees as she leaned slightly forward, her head bent and eyes focussing on her whitening knuckles; followed by a long drawn out sigh. 'I know what you are thinking . . . , why was a young lass up there by that old stone?' There was a pause and a deep intake of breath. 'The edge was where we all played as kids; knew every inch of it, and our Anna and her friends often played around there when she stayed with her gran.'

Suddenly Mr Booth found his voice, edged with great sadness and part pride. 'Our Anna was a smart child, and had a project from school to find out and write up anything of interest around the town. She had decided to research the Maidenstone.' At this point he choked back a sob.

'Did anyone else know what she had intended to do?' Lisa asked calmly.

Anna's parents glared at her for a second; then shook their heads in unison. 'Only my mam,' Mrs Booth added.

DS Pharies slid into the front seat of the police car, the last words of Anna Booth's father still ringing in her ears. 'Catch the bugger!'

Now all her instincts told her to confront Professor Wilson; but a small deep inner voice warned constraint. This time her head would rule, nothing left to chance. Although the internal struggle of wanting to go in and confront her suspect continued; she never wanted to feel the humiliation of pushing her unfounded limits again.

Detective Constable Smith turned, taking his eyes off the road for a second. 'Ok, gov.?' She nodded . . . The best respect she could ever have wished for; was that one word, gov.

'What now?' That was the only question that had left her companion's lips, as they left the car and made for the main door of the police headquarters.

She shrugged her shoulders, intent on understanding the subtle changes she now observed. Small groups had gathered; eyes and ears focussing on what was to be imparted by whoever was to be the bearer of some news. For a second she had a horrified feeling that Anna Booth's killer had probably already been arrested and where would that leave her future?

It was with considerable relief when she realized the reason for the change. Two plain clothes men, unknown to her were bending over a computer in the far corner of the room. Years of experience into recognising her own kind, told her right away that they were plain clothes officers and, as no one had talked about new recruits, it was fairly obvious they had detectives from the Manchester plain clothes division among them.

Lisa quietly made for her desk, and slid into her slightly wobbly chair, and appeared to any observer to be fully concentrated on the computer . . . , her eyes lifted from the screen as she checked the newcomers over. She tried to recall what DCI Granger had said?

Something about the dockland bombings in London by the Irish . . . or was it the Canary Wharf or Manchester? she couldn't recall, but remembered the inspector saying there was a possibility of Danesbury being a place where the bombers might be making for. Bloody hell, the words came into her head; but remained unspoken. No wonder the chief is feeling harassed with these guys around and national security a threat, she thought.

Now the two men had her full attention, the taller of the two turned, and caught her eye. 'God, he's gorgeous,' she said to herself, noting the very blue eyes and dark brows. Then as if there was mental telepathy, he turned and looked over at her; a slight smile forming.

Lisa bent her head, blushing and almost choking on a nervous cough. The writing on her computer screen appeared alien to her and slightly blurred; get a grip, her inner voice demanded. She took a deep breath only to have it expelled in a gasp as a voice uttered, 'Detective Sergeant Pharies, I presume.' He edged part of his buttock on her desk, and looked at her computer screen . . . ; somewhat puzzled.

'You speak Chinese?' he seemed impressed. Lisa gave a small chuckle. 'Needs be,' she said. He seemed clearly impressed. 'So I believe you are looking into the death of that poor young girl eh.' She nodded, as he continued. 'Well when you have time perhaps you could familiarise me with the town and the places where folks gather to gossip' . . . , he paused, 'like any new-comers in the pubs etc.'

So he's just interested in his own investigation, thought Lisa, feeling a little put out. No bloody way am I helping solve his problems with my own hanging in the balance. 'Sorry mate, I have a case of my own.'

He stood up and moved away leaving Lisa kicking herself for being so off-putting.

Now what the hell is wrong with my computer? She stared at the Chinese lettering, wondering how the Chinese themselves could make it out; before spending another half hour resetting her computer display.

The afternoon went quickly as Lisa concentrated on all the reports ever made on Professor William Watson. Most of them she had already gone through during the cold case, but soon realized there was nothing on his being sent down from Oxford in his younger years.

Lisa rolled her head around her shoulders, pushing her wheeled chair away from her desk, still staring at the screen. Pencil in her mouth she recalled Ernest's words.

She would visit the prof later. Going through it in her mind, she concentrated on being extra careful, her questions, slow and steady kept coming to mind and about taking reinforcement; Detective Sergeant Smith came to mind.

What she really needed was a confession, then an arrest would be justified; but how to make it happen was another thing.

The taste in her mouth suddenly became metallic, and she realised she'd chewed at the metal band holding the small red eraser on the end of the pencil.

Lisa spit it out, and for some unknown reason glanced over at the newcomers from the city. He was grinning, and so was his companion.

Heart thumping and red-faced, Lisa switched off the computer, picked up her keys; checked for handcuffs and stood up. Making for the coat stand, she passed Jiten's desk.

Jiten felt a hard poke in his back, and turned to see his superior giving him the go-ahead to drop everything and follow her out.

Chapter 36

'So where now?' Detective Sergeant Smith's voice was edged with resignation as his fingers tapped the steering wheel.

'Professor William Wilson,' she replied giving him his full title, whilst spilling out half the contents of her shoulder bag onto her lap. Her companion glanced down, noticing the handcuffs.

Keeping his eyes on the road ahead, he ventured in an even toned voice. 'Will there be an arrest?'

He assumed it to be a reasonable question and waited patiently for an affirmative. None came.

Jiten shrugged, accepting it was going to be just one of those days. Once again he took the now familiar roads towards the Edge. Nothing had changed, although the autumn had brought its own colours of reds and oranges; the landscape appeared little different; more barren; but still nevertheless an artist's landscape of colour shades. There was a nip in the air too, that set Jiten fiddling with the car heater.

'Warm?' he asked after a few moments. There was no reply. He turned to look at his companion, but she sat stony-faced and silent.

He shrugged, it was definitely going to be one of those days and his thoughts wandered off subconsciously to the new assistant at the Indian shop, a small outlet and a favourite of his mother's for spices for her baking needs. 'Sanita,' the name sprang to his mind; then it was gone. Lisa was talking.

'I want you to drive right up to the prof's house,' she said, 'and stay in the car until called.' Suddenly she realized what she had done and an involuntary sweat broke out. She was doing the very thing that had got her into so much trouble the last time. She forced her voice to sound normal.

'No . . . , better still, you come into the house with me.' Turning her head slightly, she tried to pick up any signal that he had cottoned on to her change of heart. If he did; he didn't show it.

Don't do anything stupid Lisa, she reminded herself for the hundredth time. This is just another interview; remember what is needed is proof. Just because Ernest said . . . , she didn't get any further with her thoughts, for there was a sharp turning of the car's wheels, as DC Smith swerved to bring the car through the entrance to the lane leading to the professor's house. Lisa found herself grabbing the edge of her seat as the vehicle bumped over the expanse of cobbles and stones. 'Bloody hell Jiten; slow down.' It was hardly worth the effort however, as he suddenly braked in front of a stone cottage.

The old planked door Lisa remembered with its strange iron door knocker was open; and in its door-frame stood the prof.

He raised a hand, in a half-hearted greeting, and then glanced down the drive, which it seemed to Lisa like he was expecting more to follow.

'So,' he said, addressing Lisa, 'what do I owe this visit from you for?' It was obvious from the look on his face he wasn't pleased at their presence, or was it just unease; contemplated Lisa.

'I just want a word or two with you sir.' Lisa put on her in-control voice and indicated inside the cottage would be more appropriate.

The prof sighed and took another quick look down the lane, before stepping aside for his visitors to enter.

'So what now, surely I cannot be under any suspicion now that the case against Betty Knowles has been resolved, tragic though it was.' He stared at his visitors; before adding, 'poor woman.'

Lisa let it go; that case was closed and she was anxious to close yet another one. 'Just want to talk to clarify a few things. 'May we;' she pointed to the chairs by the long wooden table. He nodded, and perched himself across from her, leaving DC Smith to stand by the door.

From time to time, Lisa noticed the prof's eyes darting to the clock on the wall. 'Well?' the prof sat back, folding his arms across his chest. Lisa was aware of the gesture; nothing else would be forthcoming easily.

Okay then, lets hit the nail on the head, she mused leaning slightly forward. 'Professor Wilson;' giving him his professional title. 'Why were you sent down from Oxford years ago?'

The room's clock minute hand sounded louder; emphasizing and monitoring the time before he spoke again. Suddenly the confident man before her looked old and tired. 'That's a long time ago, I was young and foolish.'

'Testing out home-made drugs?' Lisa questioned before quickly adding; 'and experimenting with no idea of the consequences.'

He nodded. 'I was immersed in the religions of the Bronze Age period, and the worship of their so called Gods, including the drugs they used during sacrifices.' He sighed. 'Yes, I was young and very stupid.'

Lisa paused for a moment . . . , 'but I believe you are now writing a book on that very subject.' She waited again for him to speak, but only got a movement of his head; indicating she was correct.

Suddenly he sighed, realizing for the first time where this conversation was leading. 'Yes, now that I have all the time in the world, I'm writing a book on Bronze Age sacrifices, and the power of myth.'

For once Lisa felt out of her depth and some contortion of her facial features must have hinted at it.

'It's about the Gods they believed in and why,' he stated, as if explaining to a student. All through the ages mankind has needed a reason for their existence and suffering.' He paused, seeing if any of this was making sense to this uptight woman in front of him.

'It's the same today. If in the future we were to discuss the belief in a virgin giving birth, we would probably laugh; but would we today, especially if you were a Christian? I find it fascinating what man can make up and truly believe in. We think the myths of the past stupid and cruel, but just stop for a moment and take a good look at the world today.'

Lisa found herself truly listening and the subject thought provoking. She began to wonder what another two thousand years would bring, and what other changes would be invented to suit mankind's comfort zones.

Jiten cleared his throat, hoping to remind Lisa what they had come for in the first place. It worked and Lisa leaned across the table looking directly into the eyes of the prof. 'Did you try out any experiment on Anna Booth?'

She waited for his reaction, then getting none, continued. 'Where were you and what were you doing when Anna Booth was killed?'

There it was out, and she awaited an explosion, but to her surprise and to her dismay none came, only another long drawn out sigh. 'I didn't even see the girl that day,' he spoke gently. 'Sorry but you will have to look elsewhere.'

There was a sound of a door opening and some movement behind Lisa. The prof looked up and paled as Lisa turned to witness the entrance of a well known figure; behind her stood the Mayor of Danesbury.

The prof pushed back his chair in an attempt to stand, but fell back again as the mayor stepped forward brushing DC Smith aside.

'This has gone far enough.' The mayor rounded the table and to Lisa's surprise, placed his hand on the prof's shoulder; as the professor seemed to sink further into his chair.

'Charlie, don't . . . ,' the professor pleaded; but a large hand stopped him by laying it on the whimpering man.

'No more hiding Bill, time to come out into the open.' Charles Chandler faced Lisa and Jiten with great dignity, which Lisa had come to admire in her mayor. 'The thing is,' he looked at the prof and half smiled, 'Bill and I are what you might call a unit.'

Put well, mused Lisa, before adding; 'but that's not what I came for.' However, the mayor had not finished.

'Bill and I were together at the time of Anna Booth's death, in fact we can confirm it as we spent the day in a hotel in Chester.' He glanced down at the prof, 'right Bill?'

The prof nodded and a tear ran down his cheek as he patted his partner's hand. 'You are a real friend.'

All this time Lisa had sat frozen in her chair, thankful that she hadn't arrested him, and doubted that they would want any publicity of the fact.

Suddenly she found her voice. 'Let's say we were never here.' She looked at DC Smith, who indicated his approval. If the prof wasn't guilty of the crime, what had his private life got to do with anyone, she mused. As for the mayor he was bloody good at his job and had done a lot for the town.

Lisa pushed her chair away and stood up at the same time as the prof moved to open the door.

'A word, lass,' he indicated a moment of her time as he walked with her to the car.

'Remember me telling you that young Chris liked to borrow my binoculars, well he still bird watches; if that's what you call it.'

Lisa moved a little closer to her informant. 'Still likes to watch.' He stared at her until he made sure she understood his meaning about only young lonely birds; never couples.

Lisa froze, fully aware of the implications. The professor turned away; walked back to his cottage and closed the door. His past behind him; he didn't want to write that sort of book anymore.

'What now,' Jiten asked. It had been a confusing day and he couldn't help feeling it hadn't finished yet.

Chapter 37

A feeling of depression swept over Lisa like a dark cloud as she struggled to adjust her seat belt.

Jitan glanced over, opened his mouth to say something positive, then quickly refrained after seeing the look on his companion's face.

Lisa stared straight in front of her, totally oblivious to the journey as her thoughts wallowed in part anger and part self-pity. The anger was directed at Ernest for sending her down a blind alley and raising her hopes for a quick arrest. Tears formed, and she sniffed. Conscious of Jitan glancing at her, she dug into a pocket for a hankie and blew her nose hard. What she needed was time to think and the thought of returning to the police headquarters brought on a flutter of anxiety.

'Drop me off at Gelsby so I can get my own car.' Her voice had an element of command; that made Jitan stiffen. Lisa sensed it and sighed.

'Have some errands to run after work and need my car,' she offered as an explanation for not going straight back with him to the police headquarters.

Once alone in the cottage, Lisa let her pent-up emotions erupt as she sat on the bottom step of her stairs; letting the tears flow. How long she'd sat there she didn't know, but it felt like a lifetime as she struggled to adjust to letting go of her preconceived ideas. Now she faced the reality of her mentor getting older; and to let go and use her own skills.

Even Jiten, who she thought fancied her, was doing a lot of shopping at the Indian store, and after glimpsing at the pretty Asian young lady at the counter; she knew why. What surprised her most; she didn't feel a thing, and was pleased for him.

Maybe she just wasn't the marrying type . . . , and that left her contemplating on what type she was and it didn't take a second to come up with the answer. She was dedicated to her chosen career, and loved every angle of it.

With that thought, her back straightened and she got up with a renewed sense of positivity and purpose.

No longer did negative thoughts plague her as Lisa drove steadily back to her chosen place of work.

There were other avenues to explore, and one particularly kept emerging to the front of her mind, but first she needed the Australian reports on Chris Knowles; call it an instinct but it was her own and not Ernest's. However this time she would play by all the rules and with great caution, for if not, there could be serious consequences.

Arriving at the police headquarters, she was met by a crowd of very angry and frightened citizens assembled outside, demanding the killer of Anna Booth be brought to justice, many holding placards;

DO YOUR JOB

NO CHILD IS SAFE

Then, as the day wore on, more and more supporters joined them; they amassed outside the Town Hall. Their anger aided by frequent trips to the pubs that were clustered around.

Detective Chief Inspector Granger and his superiors were out of their depth and it was evident from their reactions.

Anyone under them got the full force of their frustration and Lisa found herself in the middle of it all. There were even rumours of bombs being planted locally by the Irish, although Lisa failed to see what Danesbury had to offer the Irish cause apart from good stout.

In the end Lisa decided it was the final toss of the coin and if she got it wrong this time; it would be time to call it quits for any hopes of a career in the police force and she would have to move on.

The thought was depressing, and she suddenly felt very angry at where life had now placed her; and so very much alone.

It was in fact the anger that made her take the next step. Finding quiet time, it being the lunch break, she dialled Australia; the number written neatly on the top of the last e-mail she had received.

It seemed an age before she eventually got through and another age to find someone to help with her enquiry. But it was worth it. The latest Aussie report was of Chris Knowles being cautioned for his behaviour with a young girl. A new surge of optimism swept through her. The only problem was how she should now go about it. Not like last time, that was for sure, but not getting it right was even worse.

What then. Discuss it with the powers that be and leave it up to them, or take a chance and go with her gut feelings. She decided on the latter; but with the back up of her detective constable. This time she wouldn't make any rash decisions and if there was any danger to anyone; let things be. After all it was only a hunch, but a fairly good one.

The police station was abuzz with descriptions of the unrest in the town. A few constables had been jeered at and name-called, but so far no one had been hurt, although it was now clearly foreseen, if no arrests were made; things could get out of hand very quickly.

DC Smith listened patiently to his detective sergeant, nodding his head a few times watched closely by fellow officers at their desks. Lisa's own self-doubt returning; as she assured Jiten she would be treading very carefully indeed.

Half an hour later, the unmarked police car that Lisa had insisted on using, was passing the Knowles house. The drive was empty and there was no sign of the blue Accord. Six times they drove past, breaking for a quick lunch at a nearby pub. Lisa's spirits were beginning to flag; her confidence diminishing, and fresh doubts emerging.

The last time they had passed, she had looked more closely at the house to see if there were any signs of occupation. For all she knew Chris Knowles could have up sticks and left; after his mother had been arrested.

It was Jiten who spotted the cat in the window; a positive sign that the house was still occupied.

'Just drive around for another half hour,' demanded Lisa. 'Then if there's still no car in the driveway we'll call it a day.' The stress they were feeling seemed to lessen a little with the quietness and peacefulness of an autumn day in the country; which in itself proved quite relaxing, and a good break, away from all the tensions in the town.

An hour had passed before they passed the house again, this time there was the blue Accord in the driveway.

'Stop.' Lisa's voice rang out twisting her head around to make sure of what she'd seen. Jiten braked heavily; lurching both of them forward against their seat belts. He looked around for a place to park and could only see raised grassy banks and stone walls.

'Oh, pull in there,' shouted Lisa pointing to a five barred gate to a field. The two of them lifted the old gate out of a tangle of weeds and dirt and with much struggling, opened it; allowing the car to be backed in and parked.

'Hope there's no bloody sheep in the field.' said Jiten. Lisa gave him a hard look and shook her head.

Five minutes later they stood on the doorstep of Betty Knowles former home, both remembering the last time they were there; confronting a broken old lady charged with murder and her son, red in the face with anger standing behind her.

Now Christopher Knowles stood before them again, and Lisa hardly recognised him. The unkempt look was the first thing she noticed, crumpled shirt stained with food, uncut and unwashed hair; and a face badly in need of a shave. His eyes lurched first from one to the other, before he found his voice.

'What do you want now?' There was no mistaking the hostility.

'A word,' stated Lisa, one foot already inside the door, which gave the occupant no option but to step aside.

There was a smell of milk gone sour and a dark shape rubbed itself by her leg. Lisa saw the saucer of congealed milk at the bottom of the stairs.

The front room looked as if it hadn't been used since the last time she was there with Ernest.

No one sat down, but stood observing each other, and the tension could be felt like a stretched piece of elastic about to snap.

Lisa was the first to speak, and plunged in without thinking of the consequences if she'd got it all wrong. Little did either of the men present know she had already made the decision to accept the consequences, and if proved wrong; would walk away from her chosen profession.

'You killed Anna Booth didn't you?'

Whatever Jiten was thinking was kept well hidden; for this was not the right time to ask his superior about her evidence to the fact. His face betrayed no emotion, but his mind was working overtime, partly due to not having been told that an arrest would be imminent.

For a fleeting second, DS Pharies thought she might have judged it all incorrectly, but it didn't last long, as she witnessed the consequences of her actions.

Chris Knowles was looking at her with a look of almost relief. He stumbled towards the armchair that Ernest had once questioned his mother from. His head went down between his knees, hands clasped behind his head; his shoulders shook as the words came out between sobs.

'I didn't mean to, she started to scream and wouldn't shut up.'

Jiten hadn't moved and at that point felt his muscles lock. Part of him was relieved his boss had got it right; the other part angry she hadn't confided in him.

'Like the young lass in Australia?' There was no sympathy in DS Pharies' voice. 'You liked to watch young girls didn't you? . . . ,' she paused before carrying on, 'but occasionally it wasn't enough, and you wanted to touch . . .'

A loud sob came from the man. 'Just touch that's all, I didn't want to hurt them.'

'Just like you liked to touch your sister?'

A great moan of anguish came back. 'I never hurt Jennie . . . , never. It was my mum who killed her.'

Lisa sat herself down on one of the high backed chairs and leaned towards the man in front of her.

'I know that Chris, I also know you didn't do anything really bad to the young child in Australia, but you scared her . . . ,' she paused, 'Anna Booth was different I think. . . .' Lisa stopped once again before looking him straight in the eyes. 'What I think was that she made so much fuss; you just had to stop her.'

Chris Knowles looked up, his face haunted and ashen; as he nodded.

'And,' Lisa continued, 'you picked up a stone that lay near by and hit her; then realised she was dead; just like your mother had done.'

This time there was another moan of anguish as he looked at his accuser and nodded again.

'I didn't mean to, she wouldn't stop screaming.'

'But,' Lisa's voice became sympathetic and understanding, a play on her part for her victim to open up fully. 'Then you remembered how your sister was laid out and flowers put in her hand.' Lisa's voice dropped a fraction and became almost hypnotic, as she continued.

'So you laid her out beside the Maidenstone and placed a bunch of flowers in her hand, just like your mother had done for your sister.'

This time a huge guttural sound erupted, partly of relief and partly from distress.

Lisa stood up, glancing briefly over at her still in-shock detective constable, before facing Chris Knowles and uttering:

'Chris Knowles, I am arresting you on the suspicion of the murder of Anna Booth. You do not have to say anything, but it may harm your defence if you do not mention when questioned, something which you later rely on in court. Anything you say may be given in evidence.'

DC Smith already had the handcuffs out and DS Pharies was on her cell phone asking police headquarters for back-up.

Chapter 38

Lisa was totally exhausted when she at last arrived home. It always mystified her that the town itself could be in an uproar, while Gelsby remained quiet and unchanged. She gave an unconscious shrug of her shoulders verifying very little disturbed the ancient village, apart that is from gossip. However that was usually done in the local pub, or when standing around after the Sunday service was over.

As she entered the cottage she'd been born in and had lived in all her life, there suddenly came over her a feeling of emptiness and isolation. Her first thought was of the Heaths, and was disappointed they were not awaiting her with their congratulations. They must have heard it on the telly, she mused sinking into the old arm chair before kicking off her shoes. One of them flipped over into the hearth, but she made no attempt to retrieve it.

Eyes closed, head back Lisa relived the day's events; the surges of adrenaline, the success. That's who she was; that's what she craved. Maybe a psychiatrist would have a name for it, but to her it was just being Lisa Pharies.

Half turning she glanced at the telephone, then recalled Jiten saying his mother had invited some new people around. Lisa wasn't dumb, and had picked up little references to the girl Sanita, and maybe she did feel just a little jealous, but although she truly liked Jiten; she couldn't stand his mother. The unspoken admittance surprised her, but it felt like spring cleaning. That's what she needed, she mused, looking at the fading curtains and old wallpaper.

However the spring cleaning she had in mind had nothing to do with decorating; something else was stirring her adrenaline.

'I need to move,' Lisa thought, her eyes flicking to a pile of newspapers. After scattering a few of the newspapers by her feet, she found the local one with lists of houses for sale in the town.

The ones that really took her fancy and imagination were far too pricy. What she needed to ask herself was what price could she afford? And where would she like this new place to be located in the town? She ringed one or two with a marker; that just happened to be holding a dead plant upright, although she couldn't remember ever putting it there. Lisa didn't get any further with her house investigations, as she was now being interrupted by the constant ringing of her doorbell.

She jumped up too quickly, making herself a little dizzy. Ernest stood there, smiling.

Lisa frowned; as she picked up on the fact the smile seemed just a little forced.

'Well done lass.' He closed the door behind him. Nothing was said about his own conviction being off-mark about the killer of Anna Booth, and Lisa was determined not to mention it, at least not for a while anyway.

'Proud of you Lisa,' again the words were short; with no hint on how she had accomplished her actions.

'Cuppa?' it always helped break tensions; but this time Ernest held up his hand to refuse.

'Nay, Lisa.' He shook his head. 'My meeting starts shortly' . . . , he paused, 'just thought I'd pop in and congratulate you.' Ernest was looking at his watch now, and seemed in a hurry to end whatever conversation they were having.

'Guess being on the Gelsby Parish Council is going to keep you busy eh.' It really surprised Lisa just how animated her old boss seemed when she mentioned the parish council, it was as if she'd opened a flood gate of new ideas and enthusiasm for Ernest to get into.

With a little persuasion, Ernest did eventually sit down, but talked almost non stop about the mould under the church paneling, and the need for more security around the church from vandalism; which was becoming a problem for many places of worship.

Lisa half listened, and at any other time would have been thrilled to see his retirement fulfilled. But Lisa didn't feel that way at all; in fact she was experiencing a total let down; loneliness and a slight anger. She also knew the reason for her feelings. She needed, nay craved for the return of her old boss and mentor, and before she could help herself, she blurted out. 'The killer wasn't Professor Wilson.'

Ernest's eyes widened slightly, his train of thought now broken; as he focussed on the implication that he had been wrong. He thought hard before adding. 'No Lisa, I didn't say the prof. was guilty. What I said was for you to look into his past once again,' having said that, he looked a little embarrassed.

Lisa coughed and choked a little before catching her breath and couldn't help expressing another spiteful remark. 'Whatever way you meant it; it came across to me that you suspected him. So why did you want me to interview him again.'

Ernest sighed, and tried to check his watch, without making it too obvious. 'If he hadn't told you about Chris Knowles liking to spy on young girls; you might still be looking.'

Lisa's back stiffened, her eyes bright. 'I got all I needed from the Australian police.' Ernest blushed again just enough to send a quiver of satisfaction through his protégée.

'Then you have made the grade Lisa, my congratulations, I'm so proud of you.' He got up and checked his watch again. 'Must be off; things to attend to.'

Lisa stood by her front door, watching his familiar figure walk towards the church. Suddenly he seemed older, the straight back now slightly bent; his stride slower.

The Detective Inspector Heath she had worked for and revered for his case solving abilities, now became part of her past. She sighed. Change is natural; her mother would have said.

Yes her old gov. had changed. His past let go and in its place his beloved Rita, his only true love and best friend; with crosswords and puzzles to solve, and now the parish council.

Lisa gave a little smile to herself, and wondered if the man who'd asked him to join the parish council, namely Frank Butterworth, really knew what force he would be up against. Worth attending a service or two for; she mused, almost giggling.

After he'd gone Lisa felt lonelier than ever, in fact subconsciously, she realized that things had changed and there was no going back.

Her mam was dead, her childhood friends long gone, and she found herself just wanting a life that's got more to offer than an ancient village, where nothing seems to change; the biggest events, Sunday services at St. Anne's and the annual maypole dancing.

Long into the afternoon, Lisa contemplated her life style, and for the changes that wouldn't effect her job. The position which she had always strived for was to be the same as Ernest Heath in her own right.

'Detective Inspector Pharies.' She liked the way it rolled off her tongue, and was looking forward to having her next case; whatever it may be. She loved her job and she loved the town of Danesbury.

However she also needed change. The village of Gelsby was stifling her, and she knew it. Suddenly a decision was made and the scattered newspapers picked up off the floor and put back in some order; that defied any page numbering, but made sense to the reader.

Houses for Sale

Lisa stared at the black mark ringing a couple and then realised she'd already considered them before being disturbed by Ernest's visit. She gazed at the first advert and wondered if it met all her needs. It was the end house of a row of Edwardian houses, grey stone, and steps up to an imposing front door.

It also had three stories which interested her, after thinking of all the stuff she could store there; not that, in truth, she had all that much. The garden at the back was walled with a garage at the end, entered by a small alley-way.

Lisa knew the house. Years ago a girl she'd met at Girl Guides lived there and Lisa always remembered it's spaciousness, after the small cottage she had been brought up in.

Edge of town and the west end. Lisa picked up the phone. She had forgotten that the road in front of the house was now one of the busiest leading into the town. But she'd already made up her mind.

The End.